The Barry Island Murders
Andrew Peters

Published by Andrew Peters 2013
Copyright Andrew Peters 2013

All rights reserved.

Cover art by the wonderful Joe Lumley
joe-lumley@live.co.uk

Talk to me
andynpeters@yahoo.com

These cases have been transcribed from a CD found amongst the effects of retired Chief Superintendent Williams.

The only changes made have been to names, places, dates and facts.

Oh, and cutting out all the heavy swearing.

Contents

1. Journey To Mars   5
2. The Playground   45
3. The Graveyard   89

Journey To Mars

You're still trying to get exciting stuff out of me, aren't you sonny? But I keep telling you, murder investigations are rarely all that thrilling. It's generally just routine, and the most obvious suspect is usually the one that did it. Blood all over his coat or whatever. Now of course that doesn't make for great TV or a best-selling book, but most of that's all bollocks.

Bit like the spy stuff, really. I've bumped into a few "funnies" in my time, and, take my word for it, they're nothing like James Bond. Quiet, ordinary blokes, who spend years blending in, hanging around and never a whiff of glamour and blonde double-agents. No bloody invisible cars and Fanny Abundant or whatever her name was.

Same with us, we don't sit around like a game of Cluedo, waiting for some old biddy to point the finger. Can't remember a time when we all trooped down to the library with the suspects.

Once or twice someone's tried to get a little clever with us, but it almost never comes off. We're not as stupid as the lady novelists would have you believe, and the criminals are generally nowhere near as clever as they think they are. Worse still, some of them are just a little bit too clever for their own good, can't keep things simple.....like that Lady Foxborough I told you about. Always overdo things.

I suppose we did have some cases a little tougher than others.

Let me think.

I never think too well on an empty liver, mind you.

Yes, don't mind if I do. Not too much tonic.

Well, now, that's better. Let me see, this one goes back a very long way. I was just a Detective Sergeant in those days, and none of the "Williams Of The Yard" touch of my later famous years. Glamorganshire Constabulary it was then. Long before I moved to The Met.

I was working in the Saint Tropez of the Costa Del Glamorgan, son.

Barry Island.

What, never had the pleasure? It was a nice enough place back then, though I'm told it's got pretty rough nowadays. Not that I've got any plans to go back. Eastbourne will do me fine now. The wife likes it too, as it's near her sister.

What? Oh yes, Barry.

It's down on the Bristol Channel coast, about ten miles south of Cardiff. There's the town of Barry and then Barry Island, though it's connected by a decent road to the mainland. Odd little place all round, really. Used to have hundreds of old steam engines rusting away in sidings. Think they restored a few. Used to have a very busy Docks area, bringing in coal, oil and especially bananas. The Barry banana boats used to be quite famous. I dunno if the docks are still working.....most aren't in Britain any more. Not that the docks have got anything much to do with the story. Well, except for the husband.....

Yes, yes, let me get to it in my own time.

Anyway, Barry Island is where it all happened. It's a holiday resort. Nice sandy beach, long promenade, the sea as warm as you'll find in Britain and it's very popular in the summer. Or was. In fact, they built a Butlin's Holiday Camp on the headland next to the beach while I was working there. Can't remember if it was there or not at the time of the Mars case.

Well, that's what we called it. The Mars case. Nothing to do with chocolate bars or little green men, well, not really.

Wait, I'll explain.

Back to the beach. As I said, sandy, pretty long too. Usual stuff, deck-chairs, buckets and spades, people with their hankies on their heads, Horse rides for the kids. Well, you might have expected donkeys, but I only ever remember seeing horses. Little ones, ponies. In general a very pleasant place to spend a hot summer's day.

Across from the pleasure beach and the promenade, there was a row of little gift shops and fish and chip restaurants, much the same as you find at any holiday resort. Kiss-me-quick hats, rock, souvenirs of Barry, though mostly made in Hong-Kong I dare say. One rather good hotel. And the funfair.

Yes, now we're getting there. The funfair. It was a permanent thing, though I don't think it used to be open in the winter, but it was always there. Usual stuff, the waltzers, dodgem cars, haunted house, big wheel, shooting ranges, roundabouts for the little kids, amusement arcades, candy floss, ice - cream...all a bit *view jew* now with all the Eurodisney and Thorpe Park stuff, but this was back in the early sixties and it used to be very popular in the season. No shortage of visitors.

And then, of course, the cause of all the trouble.

The Journey To Mars.

It was a rickety old ride that they tarted up every year with whatever science-fiction theme was in fashion. One year it was Supercar, then Thunderbirds or Quatermass and by this time Dr Who, I think. Not that the basics changed much. You'd sit in a little car and be winched up the track inside the thing. Most of it was in the dark for the full scary effect, but lights would flash on from time to time to show you something scream-worthy. (If you were ninety years old with a weak heart maybe). I dunno, an alien, a giant spider, some green Venusian woman with four arms, and that year at least, a Dalek and a Cyberman. Every so often, you'd emerge into daylight and go down a slope that must have seemed steep back then. I think they had a water splash at the bottom of one of them.

That would look very tame indeed to today's youngsters with all the ninety mile an hour big-dippers they have, falling vertically down a hundred feet. No, no I haven't tried, but I have grandchildren who've been on them all. Damned sight braver than me, son. Prefer to keep my feet on the old *terry firm*.

Yes, pretty small beer to the modern generation I'm sure, but it was considered great fun in the sixties. People would queue up to pay their thruppence at busy times.

Thruppence. Three old pennies. God, how old are you? Bloody hell, they're sending kids out now. Anyway, more or less one new penny now. I bet you wouldn't get much at Thorpe Park for that, eh? Probably wouldn't get anything in Barry now, even if it's all still there.

So, anyway, that was the Journey To Mars. I went on it a couple of times myself. Off duty, with a girl I knew. Pauline Densley.....no don't put her name in it... I've got the wife to think of. Besides, she's probably a grandmother now. Always twenty in my memory, mind you. Of course, she'd pretend to be scared and scream, so I'd have to put my arm round her. Probably end up on a sexual harassment charge for that these days. Might still do, if she cares to make a fuss about it to one of those no win, no fee, no shame lawyers.

Well, it wasn't quite the Tunnel Of Love, but it was fun.

I can't believe it's still there for you to get photographs of, son. Health and safety probably closed it down decades ago. It was rickety enough then. Looked like someone had built it out of Meccano and then loosened all the screws. Hah!

Mecanno son......oh bugger it, never mind, just say Lego and let your readers use their imagination.

Yes, fair point, maybe they haven't. Not that I read the Mail very much.

Well, I suppose I had better get on with it, got to collect the wife from her Conservative Club meeting before too long.

It was early season as I remember, late June, maybe early July and I think it was a Saturday or Sunday afternoon, as it was quite busy, but not packed like in the school holidays. We got a call at the station about sixish to say a woman had been found dead on the Journey To Mars, so I set off down there with a Constable .... Perkins ... I think it was. Ten minute drive in one of the station Ford Anglias.... no, daresay you've never seen one of those either. Top speed just a little faster than a pushbike.

Pushbike?

Oh bloody hell, do one of them Joogle searches, son!

Anyway, we get there and there's a hell of a commotion around the entrance to the Journey To Mars. I told Perkins to call for two more constables, and get some help from the fairground management to put up some out-of-order signs and move the crowd back.

Once I could get near enough to see what was going on, I saw a woman in the front car, with some bloke leaning over her. He straightened up when he saw me and I recognised him. Doctor Rees, he'd helped us with a few things when the official Police Surgeon hadn't been available. Capable enough cove, bit flash for my tastes, but then a lot of doctors have a bloody high opinion of themselves, if you ask me. Them and bloody airline pilots, but that's another story

She was dead right enough, so he said. He thought she might have been shot, but hadn't had chance to remove her clothing to see for sure. There was a puncture wound over the heart, though not much blood, but that apparently could happen. I told Perkins to send for the ambulance and the Police Surgeon, though it appeared there was no great hurry now.

Then what to do? I'm standing inside a fairground full of people, I've got one Constable and a couple more on the way. Hardly enough to throw a cordon round the place, so I call for instructions. There's now a

Detective Inspector on the way from Cardiff. Nobody's to enter or leave the fairground till he gets here.

My arse. What hope have I got, the gates are wide open, people are entering and leaving all the time. The woman's been here half an hour already. I tell Perkins to find the management, sharpish.

Amazing how a little drink refreshes the memory, eh son? Another one wouldn't go amiss. On your expenses rather than mine.
A police pension doesn't go so far these days.

Nice.

So, the management. Turned out to be some foxy-faced little bloke. Don't know if I ever knew his name. I told him what they'd told me. Nobody to enter or leave. He just laughed. Said he'd try and lock the gates, but there were about six or seven entrances, and there was no chance of stopping people getting out if they decided to, and for sure Perkins and I couldn't be everywhere. I told him to do his best and I put poor bloody Perkins on the main gate, though I might as well have used King Canoe for all the good it did. Of course I stayed with the body.

With a Detective Inspector on the way, I didn't know whether it was my place to start asking questions, but I thought I'd at least have a word with the quack. What was he doing there, for a start.

Turned out he'd been going to meet a young lady friend for a drink and a spot of dinner in the hotel across the road. Parked up. Walking past the fairground when he hears the loudspeaker. Is there a doctor in the house.....well, the fair? Runs to fetch his bag from the car and then over to the ride. Nothing he could do, reckoned she'd been dead twenty minutes by the time he got there. Just about to call us when we arrived. He was a little worried that his girlfriend might be wondering where he was, so could he just.....?

Well, no, of course he couldn't. I wanted him there when the DI showed up. I was pretty sure I was going to get a frightful bollocking for not keeping a thousand people inside the fairground, so I wasn't going to let him slope off and start making eyes at some popsy. I had a very bad feeling that this whole business wasn't going to do my career any good at all.

I took a look at the body, of course, though since Rees had made sure she was dead, I wasn't going to touch anything. She was in the front car out of about ten or twelve, slumped over the safety bar. Brown hair was all I could see. Quite a bit of it. Wearing some patterned dress. Looked as if it came from Freeman's catalogue, but then most girls dressed that way those days. You could pay weekly, so it was pretty convenient. Used to say about the kids at school that they had so many shoes from the catalogue that they ended up with Club feet. Hahaha.

Well, you see Freeman's was a mail order catalogue you took round to your friends and it was known as the Club.....so club feet? Never mind son, never mind. I was never much of a comedian.

Anyway, patterned dress and long brown hair was what I saw, and it was about then that the DI arrived and I prepared myself for trouble.

But I struck lucky with DI Ashmore. One of the nicer policemen you'd hope to meet. He brushed aside my apologies for not keeping everyone there,

"Not your fault Sergeant Williams, what are you meant to do with one constable and all these people. Our man will be well away by now. Let's talk to the people we have got."

The Police Surgeon busied himself with the

necessary, and Mr Ashmore started with Dr Rees, who repeated what he'd told me. Ashmore asked him if he recognised the woman, but the good Doctor wasn't sure. Apparently she seemed vaguely familiar, but he saw a lot of people every day and didn't have all that good a memory for faces. Probably too busy looking a little further South if you ask me. Not that anyone did. Anyway, Rees said his bit, gave his opinions and was then allowed to leave, on the off chance that his lady friend hadn't taken the hump and stomped off an hour ago. In fact Ashmore even sent a Constable along with him to explain. Maybe just checking the Doctor's story too. Must have been a patient girl, since she was still there, and, according to the Constable, greeted the good Doctor as quite the hero of the hour. Not that he'd done anything all that heroic.

Then we had a chat with the bloke who operated the ride. He looked as if he wasn't appreciating losing business, but he had the sense not to say so. He wasn't a great deal of help. He thought the lady had been with a gent who'd helped her into the car, and then gone off to wait for her. A little unusual, perhaps, but not everybody fancies a big dipper ride. He thought it was the bloke who'd handed in the ticket, but it might have been the lady. No, for sure she wasn't dead when she went in. She sat up straight enough then. Next thing he knows is ten minutes or so later, when the cars come out for the last time, everyone gets off, but she doesn't.

He goes up to her, lifts the safety bar and reminds

her that it's only the one ride for thruppence, Lady. She doesn't move, he puts his hand on her shoulder and she slumps over. He can see something's badly wrong, so he turns off the ride and runs across to the office. They make the announcement for the Doctor, who shows up pretty quickly. He tells the people who've got into the other cars that there's been a breakdown, and they get their money back and shove off. No, for sure he hadn't heard a shot. Mind you, a funfair in full swing isn't the quietest place on Earth.

Description of the gent? Well, he didn't look too closely really. No reason to. Tallish, he thinks. Short brown hair, maybe black. Navy blue suit, or perhaps grey. No hat....or did he have one? Thirty-ish, maybe a little younger, perhaps older.

Might as well have arrested myself for all the good that was.

Meanwhile the Detective Constables had been trying to identify the deceased lady, which didn't prove too easy.

Well, it was a long time ago, sonny, and plenty of women didn't drive, and even if they did, there was no obligation to carry their driving licence around with them. Nobody'd heard of a credit card, and plenty of people didn't have bank accounts, or carry their cheque book around. There was nothing of any use in the handbag, no library ticket, Family Allowance Book or anything with a name on. Only thing of any interest in her purse was a photo of a good looking chap in Navy uniform. Merchant Navy as it happened. That was all.

Grand. An unidentified corpse, a mystery man, thousands of possible suspects and we weren't even sure how she'd died. The Police Surgeon wasn't at all convinced she'd been shot, but was keeping his powder dry until he'd done a post-mortem, or at the very least had a better look in some better light, as it was well into dusk by now. The deceased lady duly departed in the ambulance to the Barry General mortuary.

Mr Ashmore did the best he could. He ordered the whole place shut down for the day, posted a Constable at the entrance and exit to it, and arranged for it to be locked up and guarded by two more Constables. He impounded all the guns from the rifle range, though it seemed highly unlikely they could shoot someone through the heart, since they barely had enough power to knock over tin men at five yards. I knew that much from experience, as I quite fancied myself as Wild Bill Hiccough and I'd taken home quite a few prizes in my time. Mostly china dogs for Mother's mantelpiece.

Judging by some of the language Mr Ashmore used (which I daresay the Daily Mail won't want to print, eh sonny? Wouldn't want to cause "outrage" would we?), he wasn't too happy with the case at all. Something about a pig's bottom, I recall. Can't say I disagreed, but it was his problem now.

Sadly not, as it turned out.

Christ, I'm dry from all this talking.

Don't mind if I do.

Breathalyser? Don't make me laugh, sonny. They all know me around here, Williams of The Yard, they won't be stopping me. We stick together.

Wait, there's no need to put that in, is there? Just a joke, my lad. Of course the Sussex Constabulary do their duty without fear or favour. I'll take a taxi to pick the wife up, so I've room for one or two more.

Very decent of you.

Ah yes. Apparently I wasn't about to bow out of the Mars Case after all. Turns out Ashmore's Detective Sergeant was off sick.

"You seem a bright boy, Williams. I'll have a word with the Superintendent and get you assigned to me for this one. Can always use a good pair of eyes, and I hear yours are fine."

Well, I was keen enough to impress, and it looked like there might be some overtime in it. Always welcome.

How right I was. I thought it might be time to get off home, but Ashmore had other ideas. We were going to search the Journey To Mars.

Yes, that's what I thought, leave it till daylight, but he had a point, it was dark inside anyway, so might as well strike while the iron was warm. Course, they had lights inside, so we got them all switched on and started walking through, which you could do quite easily as there was a footpath next to most of the tracks and ladders to go up and down. Naturally the customers never saw any of that, just the lights to flash on for the scary bits.

Took us four hours. Four bloody hours. Checking the tracks and ground for bullet casings. Trying to find a place where a murderer could stand and get a clear shot. Well, that didn't take long, because it would have to be in one of the places where a light went on to show one of the scaries. We looked at all of them, but if there'd been a bloke with a gun in front of the Cyberman or the giant spider, surely everyone would have seen him and raised an alarm. Naturally, since she'd been in the front car we could rule out the people behind, unless she'd stood up, turned round and asked someone to shoot her.

Yes, young man.

We thought about the Dalek.

For a start it wasn't designed to open, but we got it open anyway. Hollow indeed, but if the murderer had hidden in there and poked his gun through the Dalek's sucker, he'd have needed to be three feet tall and able to seal the thing up and repaint it afterwards. It's a nice thought though, isn't it...The Dalek Murder? Not a chance.

We found absolutely nothing, and nowhere that a crazed gunman could have hidden himself, or fired from. She must have been shot as she came out.

So, four hours later, we were no further forward, and were sent off home to our beds.

Things started to get a little clearer pretty early on the following day. We'd taken some photos of the dear departed and were about to put them in the *Barry and District News*, when we were .... forestalled, as they say. In came some old dear, complaining that her daughter-in law hadn't come home last night. She was due to be back on the last bus from Cardiff after visiting a girlfriend up there. (No, sonny, a friend who was a girl.....different times....well, it might have made it more fun for your readers, but I can't help that). No sign of her last night or this morning, so the old dear was very worried.

Well, the desk sergeant took a description, and it seemed to fit our young lady from the fairground, so he showed her into my office. Can't remember what Ashmore was doing, but he wasn't there.
I asked a few more questions, got her to repeat the description, and then told her that I might have some bad news for her. Might she be able to....?

Of course.

A WPC and Perkins took her down to the mortuary at Barry General, and I assume they did the customary sheet lifting thing. Dunno, I wasn't there. I didn't have to console the poor old dear. I've done plenty of consoling in my time. All I got was the result. We now had a name for the dead woman.

Caroline .... er.... Ward, yes...Ward. Married lady, twenty-five years old. Accounts clerk for Barry Bookmakers. Husband, Colin Ward. Twenty-eight. No children. No convictions.

Yes, sounds just like I'm putting it into the files. Maybe that's the way you need to think, sonny. You'd go mad if you thought of every dead body as a living, breathing human being. Christ, the sights I've seen.

But anyway, back to the story.

So, Mrs. Ward came back into the station. Ashmore did the talking this time, and I sat there with the same WPC in case the old lady broke down. Nice girl she was...The WPC not the old lady, son. Dark hair, nice figure from what the uniform let you see. Never mind.

As I've said many times, in any case of murder we always go straight for the obvious. So we needed to have a word with that husband. Mr. Colin Ward. Where might he be found, Mrs. Ward?

Or, as it turned out, Second Mate Colin Ward of the *Regent Hawk,* an oil tanker of some size, currently three days out from Cardiff Docks, after a four month voyage out to Venezuela, via Trinidad and The Canary Islands. Or the other way around. Not important.

Which seemed to rule out the husband. Though, we were thorough enough to cable the ship later to make sure he was on board. He was. We had to tell the captain why we were asking, of course, which gave him a rather nasty interview to conduct with his Second Mate, I daresay.

Callous? Maybe, son, but someone had to break the news, and for a change it didn't have to be one of us.

Who was next on Ashmore's list?

Let's try the mother in law herself. What was her name .... no .... just Mrs Ward will have to do.

Well, we had no information at the time about how well she got on with the deceased, though she lived with her son and his wife. We asked about her whereabouts (lovely police word that, young man .... hope they still use it) at six the previous evening. Turns out she was having tea and doing some knitting with four or five friends in one of their houses on Port Road. I'll save time, we interviewed all four of them and they all swore she was there from four till six, so she had no time to sprint five miles to the fairground, take up station with a sniper's rifle and shoot her daughter-in-law as she emerged from the Journey To Mars. A tough proposition for a woman of sixty at the best of times.

Ashmore ran through the usual useless questions we have to try. Enemies? Old boyfriends? Trouble at work? Money worries? Nothing, pretty much as you'd expect. He took a few more details from the old girl and then got her taken home.

So, more shoe leather to be expended in routine enquiries. Ha! They never show you that on the TV do they, son. Probably because TV shows last an hour or two, whilst Policemen work bloody long days.

Off to Barry Bookmakers next. Let's talk to the people she worked with. Another three girls. Two on the counter, one more in the accounts department apart from the deceased, though the accounts girls could stand in for the counter girls in their lunch hour or holidays. A manager and an assistant manager, both men .... well, we are talking about the sixties. Not too many women managers about then.

Nobody was much help. The manager was fifty if he was a day, Jones or Smith I think. Spoke well of her work, but knew nothing of her private life. Or so he claimed. Mind you, he still showed up for work in a smart suit and a red bow tie, so who knew eh? Maybe he fancied his chances? We went through the routine of asking him where he'd been at the time of the murder. At home with his "lady wife" apparently. I never trust people who talk like that, but she confirmed it.

The assistant manager was a lot younger and a good looking chap, but I doubt very much if he'd have been Caroline's type....or, to be clearer, if she'd have been his ..... if you take my meaning? No, no, not at all ..... we saw things a little different back in the stone age. Mind you, as I remember, it was illegal then, so maybe she'd known something to his disadvantage? The Blackmailed Bookmaker, eh. Make a good headline that. We talked to him for ten minutes or so, but he wasn't much use. Nice enough girl, he said, but again he'd never seen her outside work. Home with his mum at six last night apparently. Probably somebody checked that, I don't remember.

On to the girls then .... they all got along well, apparently .... but never saw each other outside work. Well, I called them girls, but the oldest one must have been mid fifties and a grandmother. Bethan something ...... bit of a mother hen figure I suppose. Had nothing but good things to say about Caroline, lovely girl, terrible thing.

Who else was there .... Jennifer ..... yes ... Rose, nice young girl, not married, but courting she said, rich professional boyfriend, she'd be giving up the job soon to get married. He wouldn't want her to keep working.

And the third one .... Cunnington .... Cunningham .... Susan .... no Sally Cunningham. She was married to a chef in one of the Island restaurants. Didn't have a bad word to say about Caroline, though only saw her at work.

We talked to them together, and I seem to remember Ashmore dropping a few hints about office romances. They looked at each other, and let Bethan do the talking. Apparently Smith or Jones had been known to suffer from wandering hands from time to time, but they'd all learned to ignore it, and they were sure there was nothing serious in it.

Yes, he would have found himself in a lot of trouble these days, probably paying out thousands in compensation, but those days aren't these days. *Hautres tantes, hautres moors,* as my old French teacher used to say.

No, none of them lived in Cardiff, which ruled out the explanation the deceased had given to the mother-in-law. Well, of course we knew that already, there was no possibility that she was meeting a friend in Cardiff at the same time as she was being shot in Barry Island. So, we knew that someone was lying, either the dear departed, or her mother-in-law.

Still, I said we were thorough, so we needed to talk to everyone we could think of.

What next?

Of course, we had the operator of the Journey To Mars in again and went over his story. Nothing changed, if anything it got even more vague, but at least we had it typed up and signed.

We put something in the local paper, the *Barry and District News*, asking for anyone who'd been on the ride at that time to come forward.

We got a fair result too. Half a dozen people, all of whom sort of remembered seeing her in the front car, but none of whom took any notice of her when they were getting out. At least we could be pretty sure that there were no gunmen standing under the spotlights of the ride. Nobody heard any shots. So, she was alive going in, and dead coming out. Nobody knew how. Or when. Or who. Or why.

We did look into them all, but none of them had any connection to her that we could discover.

Yes, I suppose it is going on a while, and I do have to fetch the Missus. Perhaps we could finish this some other time?

Deadlines?

What's the rush, it's been the best part of forty years .... ah .... money I see.

Well, perhaps I could send a taxi round for the wife.....bloody hell, what's that? A talking phone? Eye Phone? Well, I am impressed .... and they'll take her all the way? Ah, yes, expenses. Well, I suppose we've got time for another one now, haven't we?

Nice

Pheuuuuufff!! Where were we? Pretty much nowhere as I remember?

Worry not, son, Williams Of The Yard was on the case. Well, yes, Williams of Barry Nick in those days I suppose. Though, as we said, it was DI Ashmore's case, but neither of us was getting very far with it. And there was a very nasty job coming up.

The *Regent Hawk* was just about to dock, and somebody would be needing to talk to Second Officer

Ward.

No volunteers at all, not that we asked for any, it was obviously our job. The DI and I both went to Cardiff to meet the ship. Up we walked, paid our respects to the captain and were shown into the Second Officer's cabin. Condolences, that sort of crap. To be honest, son, I did it for over forty years and I never got any better at it. The words always sounded hollow as I said them. Though, as a matter of fact, this time it was Ashmore who said them.

I suppose that Ward had taken the initial shock two days before. He showed no emotion that I could see. Yes, he understood that we'd need to ask some questions. No, he knew of no-one who'd want his wife dead. The mother-in-law idea was ridiculous. Of course, they'd had ups and downs, but cold-blooded murder? Never.

Then we had to get to the really nasty stuff.

Old boyfriends?

No. He was Caroline's first serious boyfriend, they'd been married three years and courting for three before that. Nobody else. Maybe she'd had a drink or two with a bloke or two, but that would all be a long time ago.

Not that unusual back in the sixties, people would be courting a lot longer before they rushed into anything. And nice young girls didn't start so young either, or gather quite so much experience. You see them sometimes in Eastbourne, pushing prams at thirteen, falling down drunk ..... no, no, you're quite right ..... let's get on.

New boyfriends?

He took that question better than I'd expected. He doubted it, she'd always seemed happy with him, though she hated the long spells when he was away. Her letters had been very regular, nothing seemed amiss. Though he seemed intelligent enough to accept the possibility. I could see him starting to think about it.

Money troubles?

Not that he knew of, they had money in the bank, the mortgage was paid ..... besides which, this was Barry, not bloody Chicago .... who was about to shoot a housewife for a debt?

We checked later, there was indeed money in the bank, no signs of any problems.

Of course the enemies question, and of course, no she didn't.

We drove him back to the house he now shared with just his mother and his memories. Told him we'd be in touch as soon as we found out anything.

Yes, son, I know it sounds unconvincing. It did every

time I ever said it to someone.

I'm getting maudlin, I know. It's the bloody gin. Make it a brandy this time. that always cheers me up. Maybe a large one.

Dead end?

No, my son, merely a short pause.

The next day we had the results of the post-mortem. Yes. I know, but things took longer all those years ago.

I won't bore you with the fine details about age, general health, all that stuff.

Just the three important points.

First of all, she hadn't been shot, though it was an easy mistake to make. She'd been stabbed with something long thin and round-pointed. Something like a knitting needle, but sharper. One thrust, straight into the heart. There wouldn't have been much blood.

Second of all, she was unconscious when she died, because she'd taken a good dose of ..... what was it .... Hydral Chlorate ... what the gangsters called a Mickey Finn.

Third of all, she'd been ten weeks pregnant.

Yes indeed, sunshine, food for thought, Useful information. Cast a whole different light on stuff.

Ten weeks, so, no matter how slow his sperm might be, it wasn't her husband. There must be a boyfriend somewhere.

Back to square one, and plenty more shoe leather to be worn out.

Just to make life easier for himself, Ashmore decided to go back to Barry Bookmakers first, and we asked a whole new set of questions. With much the same results. Nobody had ever heard Caroline speak of a boyfriend, no men had ever rung her up at work, nobody'd ever met her from work, they'd never seen her with anyone.

We gave Smith a nasty half hour down at the station.... we'd heard rumours of unwanted advances, how far had it gone .... all that stuff. Ashmore wasn't quite so nice and polite that afternoon. The poor old sod was practically in tears when we let him go.

No, we didn't seriously suspect him at the time, but the DI decided he needed a bit of a lesson. I heard afterwards that Ashmore's wife was an accounts clerk, though I'm not sure if that had anything to do with it.

Then the real tough questions. We drove up to Port Road West, the Ward house. I remember Ashmore decided to bring along a Constable as well, just in case of trouble. As it turned out, it wasn't necessary. Second Officer Ward was scarily calm all the time.

No, he had no idea that she might be pregnant. We watched him do the sums. He lit a cigarette and inhaled very deeply. I'm not a smoker myself, son, but I suppose it must be a bloody comfort sometimes, eh?

Nobody said anything for a minute.

Ashmore had to break the silence with the obvious question.

No, he had no idea who the father might be. He glanced at his mother. No, she had no idea either, though she was beginning to understand Caroline's late nights at the office and trips to see friends in Cardiff.

Ward just sat there and smoked. I've rarely seen a man so calm. Too calm, I thought. Still waters and all that, eh?

We were both pretty uncomfortable, and there seemed nothing to be gained by staying there. We made the usual noises and headed back to the station.

Am I boring you son? We could always finish another day? No, well maybe just one more. Yes, better the brandy I think.

I think that must have been the Friday, and Ashmore decided there was no point worrying at it over the weekend, so we'd take a couple of days off and have a good chat about it on Monday, unless anything new turned up. I was rather glad of that because I had plans for the Sunday.

No, not a girl, something even more interesting.

RAF St. Athan Open Day.

I doubt it's there any more, though I'm sure you could look it up. RAF base a few miles down the road from Barry. They used to hold an Open day and Air Show every summer.

A great day out it was, especially for small boys.... of all ages. They used to have a museum of vintage aircraft there .... Spitfires, Hurricanes, all sorts, but that wasn't the main attraction, it was seeing all the flypasts.

Vulcans, Valiants, Hunters the lot. At the time the number one British jet fighter was the Lightning. English Electric Lightning. Dumpy sort of thing, but with completely swept wings and the ailerons on the tips......

No, I suppose not.

But anyway, I was quite keen on planes. Used to make the plastic Airfix models in my younger days. Aeroplanes, tanks, cars, all made of plastic, and you had to stick them together with glue, then get the glue off your fingers and paint them. The planes,you're your fingers.Except I never had the right colour paints. Not much pocket money, I suppose. Still I used to have quite a collection in the bedroom Threw them all out when Mum died and we sold her house.

Long time ago now, son. I wonder if Airfix are still going? Probably not.

Yes, yes, all right!

Anyway, I was keen on planes, and I always enjoyed the air show. A great day out. That year I think I went with Pauline. She was a bit less keen than I was, in fact pretty bored and didn't try to hide it. Always a mistake to try to share your enthusiasms.

I loved it all, especially the fly past by three Lightnings. Fastest things in the British skies at that time. All ready to sort out the bloody Russians, eh? Thank God we never needed to. I think they might even have had the Red Arrows there, in their Gnats. That year or some other, I used to try and go every year.

Relevant?

No, not really I suppose, though I did see something that confirmed a little theory of mine. Confirmed it to my satisfaction anyway.

It was at the St. John's Ambulance tent that we passed on the way out. Some fat bloke had been taken ill, probably just too much sun, and the St. John's bloke was bending over him to loosen his tie or something. Couldn't really see what he was doing, or that much of the fat bloke.

No, it wasn't really one of those "Eukanubia" moments, like the old chap in his bath. I know all the best detectives have them, but not this time.

I'd been pretty sure anyway.

So, a great Sunday for me but Pauline wasn't any too happy. Moany sod she was that day. Didn't bother seeing her too much after that.

Monday morning, bright and early, Ashmore called me into the office he was using in Barry Nick. DI Brennan's office, but he was off on his holidays. Organised a cup of tea and a biscuit or two for us. It was time for a case conference he said. Just the two of us, Ashmore and me. Made me feel good that he was taking me into his confidence. Treating me as an equal. Something I've always tried to do since to my sergeants.

"So, Williams, looks pretty plain to me. What do you think?"

I told him what I thought, and it was pretty much the same as what he thought. Trouble was, how were we ever going to prove it?

You see, my lad, that's the bloody difference between the crime paperbacks and real life. In the books the little Frenchie or the old granny explain it all in the library, fling a sudden accusation at the guilty party, who laughs at them and says something stupid like.

"But I was wearing gloves."

Chief Inspector Thicke shouts, "Aha," slaps on the cuffs, drags him away and he's locked up, tried and hanged in the last three paragraphs.

Not anywhere near that easy in real life. For a start all eight suspects in that library would have had solicitors present, telling them to say nothing. And we poor sad policemen have to come up with incontrovertible evidence to convince a judge and twelve good men and true. That's by no means as simple as the books would have it.

Yes, alright good women too these days. No, I didn't know that seventy percent of your readership were women. Ask me if I give a stuff?

No, no, fair point, maybe a brandy too many. Sorry, I'll take a deep breath.

Anyway, we couldn't do it. Couldn't get the proof. We asked everyone we could think of, we went to all the obvious places, we showed photos of the two of them.

Nothing.

They'd been bloody careful. Wherever they'd met, it had been nowhere near Barry .... or if it had, they'd made sure that they were unrecognisable. No hotels, guest houses, parks or even bloody fairground rides remembered seeing them together.

We took the obvious route of course, and one day when he wasn't around, we demanded to see the records. Bingo, three years earlier, we could put them in the same room for ten minutes.

It still wasn't enough to build a case.

Well, remember, these were the dark ages. We had none of that DMA stuff. We could tell who definitely wasn't the father of her baby, but anyone of fifteen million people in Britain still had possibly the right blood group.

But we knew.

We had him in. Of course we did. Naturally we couldn't beat it out of him, even back in the dark ages, but we could at least try to make him sweat, make him give something away.

Went over it time and again. Ashmore seemed friendly enough, but he was after him, plain enough. Tried to keep at him.

Yes, he had seen her that once, but could hardly be expected to remember it amongst so many. No, he'd never seen her since. We'd seen the appointments books. Nonsense, how could we think ..... and at that point his solicitor suggested he stopped answering questions, since we clearly had no basis for a charge. And, of course, he was right.

Yes, of course it was the bloody quack, who else?

I've no idea how a ten minute consultation had progressed to an affair, but I'm bloody sure it did. Must have met somewhere else after, but I'll never know. No idea when she told him she was worried about being late, and I'm bloody sure he didn't check her out in his surgery. Somewhere or other a little more private.

You want to know what I think? I think he invited two women down for dinner that night, met Caroline an hour before the other, and bought her a drink. Slipped the Hydral Chlorate or whatever into it and, once she was good and unsteady, took her off to the Journey To Mars. Waited ten minutes, heard the appeal for help for the poor unconscious bitch, then went across there, leaned over her and stabbed her while everyone else was being ushered away. I dunno what he used, but we had no chance of finding it now.

That's what I think, sonny, and I think he'd have got away with it if he hadn't been such an arrogant, overconfident swine. Why bother with the stabbing part? All he needed to do was slip her something a little stronger, put her on the ride, and when she'd come out poisoned to death, we'd never have been any the wiser. But no, he had to over-elucidate, sonny. I tell you, when we searched his house afterwards, it was full of crime novels ... Christie, Sayers, Allingham, Marsh ... all those fiendishly complicated plots. He couldn't just keep it bloody simple. He'd have gotten away with it otherwise.

No, you misread me sonny. It never came to trial. We gave it everything we could to try to build a case, but it was all too circumstantial. The Superintendent talked to the Public Prosecutor's office, but they said it wasn't enough. We had to give it up.

Next thing we knew he'd done a bunk. Didn't turn up for work one morning, and the receptionist couldn't get an answer from his house. We went round, but the place was deserted. Naturally enough, we had no idea if he'd taken suitcases and clothes. Maybe he thought the game was nearly up. We put out an alarm for him, but never got any results.

And then one morning we had a call from the Docks Police.

They'd found a body.

Pure coincidence, a Banana Boat had hauled up its anchor and dragged up the remains of someone. Attached to an iron weight.

Yes, it was indeed the good Doctor Rees, though it took his dentist to identify him. Or maybe they just did it from all the Brylcreem on his hair. Joke,son. Apparently the guilt must have been too much for him to bear, and he'd tied his feet to the weight, with some strong sailor's knots, and jumped into the docks. Probably the dent in the back of his head was caused by the anchor.

Seemed a good enough explanation for DI Ashmore, so it was certainly good enough for me and the coroner. Not that anything about the Journey To Mars came up at the inquest. Turned out the good Doctor had quite a few money worries too. "Suicide while the balance of his mind was disturbed," was the verdict.

After all, what other explanation could there be, unless someone had gone round and told that calm husband of hers his pet theory.

And who on earth would do that, eh, sonny?

Alright then, just the one more.

The Playground

Another early case then, young man? You think your readers might be more interested in that than in my "Williams Of The Yard" days? Can't really see why, Barry was a small enough town, no bloody serial killers or exciting murders there. All the serial killers live in Scotland according to the books I see. Must be all that bloody rain and haggis, drives them mental.

Mind you ...... there was that one case....

Dunno, my memory isn't what it was....perhaps a glass of the old memory restorer.....maybe a large one....

Ah...that's better....energise the little green cells as my chubby old Belgian friend used to say.

Now, where were we?

Yes, the Playground Case, as we called it, for pretty obvious reasons.

I think it was probably the first case I dealt with once I'd got my promotion to Inspector. That DI Ashmore must have put in a few good words for me. Youngest Detective Inspector in Wales, apparently. Last bloody surviving one now, I shouldn't wonder. So that must have made it '64 or '65...I suppose you can look it up, it was a pretty famous case at the time. Famous in Glamorgan anyway. Never had a lot of serial murders down there. Not that this one was really like the books they put out now. Nobody was sending me body parts, and I wasn't an alcoholic.

Really.

Alright, alright, let's see if we can get the facts in order.

I was asleep when it all started. I'd been out the night before with a young lady of my acquaintance ......Anne ...Anne Davies. We'd been to the pictures, and then for a drink or two before closing time. Hah, the pubs used to close at half past ten in those days. Well, maybe I have told you that before, I'm an old man sonny.

Then I'd walked her home.

Never you bloody mind whose home!! Cheeky young sweep.

Anyway, I was sound asleep at about seven that morning when the phone went off. Still remember the number, "Barry 2943," that's how you used to answer the phone ... give your number, not your name.

Jenner Road Nick. Well, who else would it be at that time of the morning. Somebody's found a body in the kids' playground behind the town hall. Car on the way to pick me up (they knew I didn't like driving if I could avoid it), be there in ten minutes.

Just about time for a quick splash and to get dressed. No time to shave, but I wasn't looking too bad as I'd had an extra one the previous night for Anne. Always the gentleman. Always had shirts ironed in the wardrobe, used to do a fresh batch every Sunday night while I was watching "London Palladium," assuming I could get a decent picture on the old steam telly.

"London Palladium?" It was a variety show, son. Dancers, comedians, singers a load of dead people you'll never have heard of.

And Bruce Forsyth.

Anyway, I'm finishing knotting my tie when the squad car pulls up outside. Vauxhall Victor I think it was that year ... I'm sure you can find a photo of one to put with the story.....though maybe it's not that important. Nice WPC driving I seem to remember, dark haired girl, from what could be seen under the regulation cap. Hair up, of course. A police uniform never displays the female body to its best advantage, it has to be said. You used to get a nice surprise seeing them off duty, mind you. Yes.

What?

Oh, right, yes, she drove me down to the town centre. Pretty empty at that time on a Saturday...yes, I remember now, it was a Saturday. King Street I think it was, just behind the Town Hall, there used to be a kiddies' playground. No idea if it's still there now. No idea if the bloody Town Hall's still there, come to that.

Yes, kiddies' playground. All the usual stuff they used

to have . Swings, slide, roundabout, see-saw. And one rather unusual thing.

A dead bloke lying at the bottom of the slide.

I couldn't see him too well, since the Police Surgeon was bent over him. presumably certifying that life was extinct. I bloody well hoped so, since I'd been dragged out of bed to deal with it. There was a constable or two about and also my Detective Sergeant, who'd shown up about the same time as me. What was his name ..... Davies. Yes, Bill Davies.

Yes, I know that was the girl's name ten minutes ago, son. Trust me, there's more than one Davies in Wales.

Well alright, I'd hate to confuse your readers.....call her Anne Hughes or Jones or something. She doesn't come back into the story anyway, so it makes no difference. Fair play, she's got damn all to do with it, so you can leave her out completely.

Gawd, you do distract me when I'm trying to tell a tale. son.

So, DS Davies was able to fill me in without my getting too near to the *corpus delightful.* Believe you me, I've seen quite enough of them. Well, not all that many then, but plenty since.

Apparently it was an old boy, running to fat, looked about sixty-five to him. First indications were that he'd been stabbed. Probably been killed somewhere else and then placed on the slide, since there wasn't much blood there.

Well, I supposed that made more sense than the idea of a fat pensioner climbing up a kids' slide and whizzing down, only to be met by a mad knifeman. Though I hadn't got as far as making sense of anything at that time in the morning.

As usual, there was no identification to be found. Most of us never carried any (well, yes, alright, the police had their warrant cards) but it seemed that this gentleman didn't even have a wallet on him. Or, more likely, he'd had one, but someone had removed it.

Squeamish or not, I needed to take a look.

I wandered over to the slide, nodded at the Police Surgeon ..... don't remember his name....and took a look at the dear departed. An old boy indeed. Pretty much dressed in the old boys' uniform. Grey trousers, highly polished black shoes, white shirt, blazer with some kind of regimental badge, and some tie or other that also looked pretty regimental. I'd have staked my pension on his being ex-military, though I didn't recognise the badges. Sixty-five seemed a fair enough guess. and I had to agree that he was a little bit out of training. Fat might have been unkind, but probably accurate. Happens to us all as the years go by, I suppose .... could do with losing a few stone myself.

I asked the Surgeon what he thought. Cagey as ever, until he'd had a chance to take a good look, but it appeared our friend had been stabbed through the heart. Might not have been a lot of blood shed, but probably a little more than there was on the slide. So maybe the deed was done elsewhere. Quack thought he'd been dead about nine hours. So, around eleven last night.

I suppose it was time for me to do some detecting, so I took a closer look. I detected that he was indeed dead, but not much else. I took a look at his shoes. Military polished, as I said, but the heels were scuffed, with a little wear. As if, for example, someone had dragged him backwards across concrete.

Call me Sherlock.

Bugger me. You've heard of him son? Miracles will never cease.

Fact is, I was looking for it. Given that he wasn't the type to be going down slides in the small hours, someone must have put him there. Either two people, fore and aft, or one dragging him. Looked like a one-man job.

Sorry son, don't mean to be sexy, maybe a one woman job .... though the corpse was a serious lift at sixteen stone. Well. that was a guess, but whatever he'd died of it wasn't anorexia .... not that they'd invented anorexia back then.

A dead pensioner on a playground slide. Odd enough to start with. The fingerprint boys were there, showing no enthusiasm at all for sprinkling talcum powder all over a bloody slide, but I decided to let them earn their money. Couldn't be more than a couple of thousand sets of prints under the rails. No, no, forget it, young man, it never did come to anything.

So, witnesses?

A Mrs. Joan Thomas, out walking her dog early in the morning. She'd walked past, the dog had snivelled, and she'd taken a look to her left. Hadn't gone in, just headed for one of the phone boxes in King Square and dialled 999.

Bloody dog walkers. They always discover the bodies. I was all for locking her up straight away. Especially since they hadn't invented joggers than. They're the other buggers who're always coming across bodies. Arrest them all!

Another of my jokes, son....it just seems they're the only people who ever discover bodies. Alright, alright, let's move on.

Of course we took a statement from Mrs. Thomas, but it seemed unlikely she was involved. She was about the same age as the deceased, but half his weight, so she'd have struggled to drag him to the slide, wait ten hours or so and then call us down to interview her.

Call it my copper's nose, son, I just didn't see her as the guilty party. Of course, we probably did the thorough thing and checked her. Made sure she wasn't his first wife or some such. Which, apparently, she wasn't. But you always have to check. That's the thing about proper coppering, son, you never take anybody at their word, you check everything. So we did.

Nothing.

But let's come back to where we were, son. A fat middle-aged bloke, stabbed to death halfway down a slide in a kids' playground.
No idea who he was, no witnesses, no motive, no ideas.

What a job.

Still, we did all the normal things, the body was packed off to Barry General, the fingerprint boys were left there and we buggered off back to Jenner Road station for a cup of tea and some Nice biscuits (Well, I was a DI now, I'd moved up in the world). I shared them with DS Davies .... Phil I seem to remember his first name was, or was it Bill after all......... not that we were big on first names in those days. If you were the superior officer it was "Sir," otherwise it would be surnames only. Yes, probably is very different these days. I don't work there these days.

We were there about half past nine, thinking that

we'd have to start putting advertisements in the *Barry And District,* when the desk sergeant knocked on my door. Apparently there was a lady, come down to report a missing husband.

Show her in Sergeant Linane, says I. And in comes the lady.

Have you ever seen a lady in her mid-fifties, looking much like any other? That's what she looked like.

Yes, it's a funny thing, back in the sixties, a woman of that age always looked like somebody's grandmother. These days they go down the gym, have the surgery, get the Bollox injections and the lippofaction and they look like ..... well, to my mind, son they look like orange Martians .... but what do I know?

Anyway, I'm not here for my descriptive skills, young man. In she came. Another Mrs. Thomas (I can't help it, son, we were in Wales! I know all the best books have a different name for each character, but I'm not writing fiction.). Seems her husband Graham hadn't come home last night. Been to some sort of reunion or other, she had no idea what, and never came back. She'd waited up till eleven. then gone to bed and dropped off. She'd woken up alone this morning, panicked and called us. Someone suggested she pop in, and so she had.

I sat her down and called in a WPC. Always a good plan in case some woman goes to pieces on you. I think it was the same girl who'd driven me down to the playground. Dark hair, What was her name? Langford, or something. Doesn't matter. Anyway, she sat there and said bugger all. DS Davies was there too, of course.

Now Mrs Thomas, Can you give us a description of your husband?

Sadly much the same as the deceased. Five foot ten, fifteen stone, (give him the best of it) last seen wearing a pair of grey slacks, a Welsh Guards Blazer, Welsh Guards tie and a 'Jim'll Fix It' badge.

Sorry son, sorry..... you're right, I really will never make a comedian.

Much the same description as the dear deceased that we'd found a few hours ago. I do the sad faced thing and invite her to pop down Barry General with DS Davies and WPC Langham to see if there's a dead body there that rings a bell.

No son. Of course I didn't express it in those terms, but I didn't want to be there. I've told you before, I don't much like to witness these things. Call me cold, call me what you like, but I've just seen way too many of them. Let me just stay cold and uninterested, otherwise who knows how mad I might go? Be fair, son, How many dead bodies have you had to unveil while the nearest and dearest stood over them?

Thought not.

Whatever, about an hour later, Mrs Thomas was back in my office, having identified the deceased. Yes indeed, Colonel Graham Thomas, MM DSO & Bar. Served all through the war, in with the invasionary force at Normandy. Retired from the British Army in 1960 after thirty-five odd years of honourable service, with a full pension and some mild arthritis.

According to Mrs Thomas, he'd gone out the previous night with some old army friends, for some kind of reunion or other and never came home.

Well, of course we had some questions to ask, and we tried to ask them as gently as possible.

What sort of reunion?

She didn't know really, she thought it might be with his military friends, since he was wearing his Welsh Guards tie and blazer. But then those reunions were normally up in Cardiff, and she hadn't been listening all that carefully, since her daughter was due to come round and drop the baby off for her to sit, since her daughter and her husband were off to the Theatre Royal to watch a James Bond film what was it called Goldenfingers or something like that, but she wasn't sure……

She was in no state to be answering questions, so I got the WPC to drive her home and arrange for someone to come round and stay for a bit. I think it was the daughter.

So we had no idea where the reunion might be, though it probably wouldn't be too hard to find out. If it was a Welsh Guards reunion that he'd been to. I had no idea at this point, sonny, though it seemed to me that the Welsh Guards probably weren't in the habit of stabbing each other too much at their annual reunions.

But as I keep saying, police work is all to do with crossing the whatsits and dotting the thingummies. Putting in the shoe leather, checking everything. And so we did.

Yes indeed, there was a Graham Thomas on the electoral roll, formerly resident at The Larches, King Street. No criminal record,

Then we got in touch with the Welsh Guards. Wasn't difficult, amazing what the phone book will do. That's where we started to draw a blank. No reunions last night, in fact none at all for the next few months.

Whilst I was at it, I got them to look up Graham Thomas in their files. He had indeed been awarded the medals mentioned, pensioned out of the army with the rank of Colonel. and. apparently. Lived a blameless life ever since.

So, why would anyone want to stick a knife in a retired Colonel from the Welsh Guards? Admittedly his wallet was missing, but most people in the sixties never carried enough money around with them to make a robbery worth while, Couple of pounds at most, and the fashion for street robbery hadn't reached Britain at the time. Another present from our American friends. According to his wife, he would have been unlikely to have had more than a fiver on him, probably cashed a cheque for that much in the afternoon to buy a few drinks for the boys.

So, once again, we were pretty much nowhere, waiting for a report from the Police Surgeon after the post-mortem, and perhaps a few witnesses from the street.

To which end, we put the customary photo in the *Western Mail*, and *South Wales Echo*, asking for witnesses....had anyone seen this man, all that rubbish. And the *Barry And District*, of course Desperate hope, since we already knew pretty much who he was. Still, that's the system, eh, young man?

So, as with all these cases, progress takes a while. We had no witnesses to the evil deed so far, so the first thing we needed to do was find out where he'd been that night. It seemed it was some kind of reunion, but evidentially not the Welsh Guards, so what..... or whom .... or which? Well, these days, you'd press the Joogle button and find out in ten seconds, but back then things took a lot longer. I sent some constables down to Barry Library (next to the town hall, as it happens) to look through the back issues of the local paper and see what they could find.

Not much, as it turned out. There were no military reunions scheduled for the previous six weeks. Army, Navy RAF. Nothing. Then I sent some constables round all the pubs in the town centre with his photo. He'd had a drink or two somewhere, so probably someone would recognise him. Nobody seemed to. He wasn't a regular in any of them, and no-one remembered him from that night.

We spent a day not getting very far.

Alright then, it was time to talk to the widow again. Never a job I relished, but it had to be done. DS Davies got the job of coming along, and we took the WPC with the dark hair too. As I said before, if you're asking questions of a woman, it's always best to have another one along, just in case.

King Street then, A nice white detached house as I recall. Sorry to have to bother her and all that, she understood how things were, we needed to ask some questions, hoped they wouldn't upset her......

Of course, she understood .... anything she could do to help .... not that she understood what .... or why.....

Well, of course, we ran through the list of rubbish questions we always ask.

Enemies?

Bollocks. Well, that wasn't what she said, but for Christ's sake .... who has bloody enemies?

Girlfriends?

Well, fair play she gave it some thought, then just smiled. The man was well over sixty, not exactly a magnet for the young ladies, not really stinking rich. Mrs Thomas didn't think so. She couldn't see some jealous husband slitting his throat after he'd been paying too much attention to a young wife. Nor could I (though I didn't miss the "slitting the throat" bit .... might be a double bluff, though I doubted it).

She had no idea, and she was desperately upset. The man she'd been with all her adult life had been murdered, she had no idea why, or who, and she was faced with the bloody nasty prospect of spending her remaining years alone and bereft. For sure, she'd had nothing to do with it, as far as I could see.

We left it and went back down to Jenner Road.

By a miracle, we had the post mortem report ready. I suppose they weren't too busy that week.

Not that it helped too much.

Stabbed indeed, twice through the heart with something long and sharp, As it turned out, either one would have been enough to kill him. Looked like he'd been dragged backwards onto the slide, judging by some bruises under his arms (And the scrapes on his heels, spotted by Hercule Williams!).

Most of the rest was a doctor's report on the state of his health .... a drinker, a smoker, a serious eater ..... his prospects might not have been good, but that didn't mean that some bugger was entitled to curtain them, eh sonny? If every one of us old boys who weren't looking after ourselves too well were due a stabbing, then I wouldn't be sitting here talking to you and pointing out that it's your round.

Nice one, son.

It seemed I was due no sleep that week. Must have been around eight on the Thursday that I got another one of those bloody phone calls.

Dead body, floating in Cold Knap Lake ..... car would pick me up in fifteen minutes. I was getting used to the instant rising and dressing stuff, and I even had time for a shave this time. I hadn't been out the night before, so I probably needed it..

Cold Knap? Well, quite an upmarket part of Barry. A beach, but this one wasn't so popular, since it was covered in pebbles rather than sand. Actually the sight of quite a famous law case, after some bloke hired a deckchair and it split under him. He won lots of money I think. Castleton v Barry Urban District Council. Quite famous indeed .... though the only reason I know about it is a night I spent with a young solicitor's clerk .... you can leave her out of it.

Cold Knap was famous for two things, the Barry Lido open air pool, and the lake, in the shape of a Welsh Harp. Boats for hire, you could row around it all day if you felt like. I'm told the lido is long since gone, but the lake is still there. I dunno, never been back in forty tears.

But anyway, none of this is of any importance. The WPC with the dark hair .... what was her name .... Joan?.... shows up and drives me down there. As usual I turn up halfway through, behind a couple of constables, both rather damp, and DS Davies. Good old Bill. Or Phil.

Dead male, found floating in the lake when the caretaker showed up this morning around seven - thirty. Surprise, surprise, no dog walkers involved. Twenty feet offshore, though hardly a problem to drag him in as the top depth was only about three feet. "Lake" it was called, but pond would probably have been a better word. I sent the two damp constables back to the Nick to warm up and change,

So, he'd been dragged ashore, and the Police Surgeon was with him now. For sure, he was dead, one way or the other. Another old boy. according to Davies. Grey slacks. Jacket. Tie.

I was beginning to find this rather nasty.

Well, young man, I think I'll be needing to get off now. The wife will be expecting me home for dinner, and there's quite a bit of this to get through yet. Shall we say Tuesday? Same time same place? The Mail is still interested I assume? No point my coming up here every week and bleating on if they aren't going to print it, eh??

See you then ..... no ..... no, I'm fine to drive.

So, where we were, young man? Just about at the point where you fetched me a brandy and soda I think?

Nice.

Ah yes, the body in the Cold Knap lake. Well, it'll probably come as no surprise to you that there was no wallet to be found and no identification on him either, So we were stuck with that "Elderly male running to fat, no distinguishing marks," idea once again. Really no distinguishing marks this time, since he hadn't acquired a stab wound or anything life threatening. According to the Police Quack, he'd probably drowned, but he couldn't be sure ... blah, blah, blah.

Thought he'd been dead about eight hours at a first look, though the water made it much more difficult to be exact. Well, that seemed reasonable, since, I daresay, most of the people who'd hired boats the day before might possibly have noticed a corpse floating around the lake, no matter how keen they were on impressing their girlfriends. I took as look at his shoes too. Somebody'd dragged him backwards into the lake. Or he'd been riding his bike and stopping it with his feet on the ground. I knew which one I favoured.

You're getting bored with this, I can see, son. Can't help that, it wasn't as if we could come up with instant answers all the time. Off went the deceased in an ambulance to Barry General. It was back to Jenner

Road for a think, a cup of tea and some routine stuff. No doubt it would have been a fag as well for most of them, but I never did learn to smoke. DS Davies and that nice WPC did. Wished I could have offered her one or lit it for her. Felt I was missing out on the smokers' camaraderie, but it wasn't me. Always looked rather romantic in the old films. Bogart and Bacall. Bette Davis and wassaname....

I'd probably just have burned my bloody fingers trying, eh?

So, we had two old boys dead inside a week, for no reason that anyone could figure out, in rather odd places. It was beginning to sound like some cheap detective novel. "The Mystery Of The Old Buggers," or something like that, except that it was no joke, and we certainly needed to find out who the body in the lake was.

Not too difficult as it turned out.

Once again, we were at the stage of talking about taking photographs and putting them in the papers, when a lady came in. Well, why not ..... if your husband's gone missing unexpectedly, why wait?

Mrs Dr. Charles Bynon was this lady's name, so you'll probably guess that her husband was Dr. Charles Bynon. Medical Practitioner. According to her, he'd gone out for a drink with some friends the night before, and never shown up at home.

You'll understand the routine by now. I sent DS Lewis and that brunette WPC down to Barry General with her to do the sheet lifting stuff.

They were back pretty soon. Yes, of course it was him. Dr Charles Bynon. GP up at Holton Road.

Mrs Bynon seemed to take it very calm. Sometimes they do, then go to pieces afterwards. I thought I'd take advantage and do all the proper Police stuff at her now while she was here..

Where had he been?

Some drink thing with some friends, he'd been due back at eleven. no, nothing special, just some old pals. No idea where they were going, but he hadn't taken the car, so it might not have been too far. They lived out on Cold Knap, opposite the bottom end of Romilly Park, more or less.

Had he been a military man? Apparently not, too young for the first one and too old to be called up for the second. Besides, as a doctor, he was more use at home. She supposed he might have done National Service, but long before she'd met him. I didn't even know whether they'd had national service in the twenties, but I supposed someone could find out for me. The blazer badge was from his golf club, it turned out.

The enemies nonsense?

No, what a surprise, no sworn enemies bent on revenge.

Old girlfriends? New girlfriends?

Be serious, look at the man. Her words, not mine.

Did he like bloody swimming? Especially at midnight?

Alright, we didn't ask that one, but nearly. We were getting too desperate. Two old boys dead in two days and not a bloody clue.

Well, nothing much we could do, except have the Widow Bynon taken home in a Police car and assure her that we'd be in touch as soon as we found out anything. The usual rubbish. And I told the WPC to get a photo of the deceased.

Back to the routine stuff again. Constables were sent round all the pubs on Cold Knap with the photo. Had he been in, who with, what time did he leave, did he seem unsteady on his feet?

This time we got an answer pretty quickly, and Lewis and I headed down to the Cold Knap Hotel. Big place, built on the site of a dance hall that had burned down in the fifties, so not as old as most of the buildings around.

It was around three by then, so they were just about to close for the afternoon .... yes, good old British licensing laws. The manager offered us a drink, but there was that "on duty" thing again, so a couple of glasses of lemonade sufficed.

We talked to the barman, who'd been working the previous night too. No idea of his name, he wasn't guilty anyway. Yes, of course he remembered Dr Bynon being there. He was a fairly regular visitor. Most Wednesdays he thought. Been in with some of his friends ..... Mr Edwards the manager of Williams and Glyns (bank, son) and Tom Cartwright, who'd been a solicitor till he'd retired. They'd all had a few drinks, gin and tonic for the Doctor. No, he hadn't been drunk, it was only three or four and the Doctor had a good head for it. They'd left at closing time, so half past ten, give or take ten minutes.

A drive to Williams and Glyns bank seemed indicated, and we just had time to get there before they closed for the day if Lewis looked sharp, which he did. They were just closing the door when we arrived and flashed the warrant cards. Smart bloke on the door, he shut it in our face while he called the Police Station. I wasn't too happy, but better safe than sorry for a Bank.

I'd not met Geoff Edwards before. Smallish bloke, coming up to retirement I suppose. Of course, he was desperately shocked by the news. Only been drinking with the bloke last night, and here he was dead. He pretty much confirmed the barman's story. The three of them had left around quarter to eleven, Edwards and Cartwright had gone one way, and Dr Bynon had walked off in the other direction towards his home. Past the lake, yes, of course. No, he'd had a few, but he was nowhere near drunk. Fall in the lake? Bloody ridiculous, of course not.

As an afterthought I mentioned Colonel Thomas' name from King Street. Didn't seem to ring any bells.

We got Cartwright's address out of him and drove back to The Knap. Lovely big house. Well, you don't see many poor solicitors, do you? Another old boy in his sixties, this case was full of them. I won't bore you with the details, but he confirmed the bank manager's story word for word. He claimed not to know Colonel Thomas at all. Either they'd both killed the good doctor together, or they were telling the truth.

No. I didn't ignore the possibility, young man. Stranger things have happened, though not many in my experience. Still, I gave the barman another try later on. No, no argument between the three of them, old friends they were. He'd seen them leave, but he hadn't seen which way they'd gone.

The two of them might have been lying, but it seemed a remote chance.

That was enough for one day. Lewis dropped me at the Station and I drove home. Last I saw of him he was having a smoke with that WPC. I swore I needed to take smoking lessons.

So, what day was it next, son? Friday? Arsed if I know either, but I dare say you can sort it out. I drove down to Jenner Road....think it was a Hillman Imp, can't really remember ..... but I hated driving. Always have, but generally needed to.

I walked into my office, had to walk past DS Davies and that WPC smoking in the corridor. Bugger all that. Get in here, Davies this is a murder case we need to talk about.

Sorry Sir.

Well I felt a bit guilty, it wasn't his fault ..... maybe I just fancied the WPC .... but anyway, we had business to sort out.

I apologised for snapping at him, pressure of the case. He said nothing, just waved a hand. So, where were we?

Practically nowhere. Two old boys dead and no seeming connection. It was time to find a connection. I put Lewis on to a thorough check of both men. Birth certificates, schools, places they'd worked, army service, anything he could find. He'd be needing to visit the widows again, which I didn't envy him. I gave him DC Perkins to help him.

I don't know why not, maybe she was busy on something else.

Anyway, Lewis had plenty of work ahead of him.

These days he'd probably just ask his magic computer, but back then everything was on paper. And in lots of different places. Researching someone's life history was no easy task. Keep him out of mischief for a few days.

What was I doing? I think I was due in court that afternoon, some remand hearing or other, I think. Dunno, some petty case or other, theft, burglary. Nothing to make headlines anywhere, much less interest your readers. Think I might have gone out for a drink or two with that Ann. Early night, no chance of a weekend off with some lunatic on the prowl.

Saturday dawned and off to work for me. Mercifully no early-morning call to come and find a pensioner halfway up a tree or anything.

We'd managed to find the sum total of zero witnesses who'd seen anything suspicious either night. Or if they had, they weren't rushing forward to tell us. Hardly surprising I suppose. With the pubs closing at half past ten, most towns were pretty quiet at night back then. People didn't use to go out so much, far fewer of them had cars, so they were at home, tucked up in bed by eleven. The TV used to close down early too, so there wasn't much to keep them up. I remember they used to play the National Anthem at closing down time. The English National Anthem, of course.

Post mortem results came through. Well the early stuff anyway. Death from drowning, though it appeared that he'd taken a good bang on the back of the head as well. Some bruising on the back of the neck too. Perhaps somebody'd smacked him one, dragged him to the lake and then held him under. Sounded like a man's work to me, or a bloody strong woman.

Not quite the same *modo operatico* then, but enough similarities to be going on with. Either there was some nutter targeting retired blokes in blazers, or there must be some connection that we couldn't see. I badly needed Lewis to turn something up.

Though, as it turned out, I didn't.

Because I had a phone call that afternoon.

Major Dodd his name was, he'd seen the *Barry and District* and knew Colonel Thomas well, felt he could shed some light on things. No, he couldn't pop up to the Station, couldn't walk, could we drop down and see him?

Lewis was off somewhere chasing up birth certificates or something, so DC Perkins and I took a Ford Cortina (not a squad car, son, we were CID) and drove up to Romilly Road to see the Major. Lovely big house, overlooking the park. Must have cost a lot of money. Most of them on that road ended up as flats, but this was all his.

Military man for sure. He would have stood up ramrod straight, if he hadn't been sitting in a wheelchair. Introductions were made and then his man wheeled him into the lounge. Corporal Blair. apparently. Big bloke, Forty odd I supposed. Been with him ever since the war, The Major told us, first as batman, now as general tacfotum. The Major had been blown up in Aden, he never got up from the chair now. Sorry to hear it, not that it seemed exactly german to the task at hand.

There was an offer of tea.... or something stronger .... but we were on duty, and just got down to it. Shame, I could have done with a nice little drop of something.

Yes, he knew Graham Thomas, had done ever since they were at school. Desperate shock to pick up his local paper that afternoon and find out he was dead. No, Corporal Blair always went shopping on a Saturday morning and picked up the local rag then. He never bothered with any of the dailies.

Yes, there'd been a little reunion on Wednesday night but nothing to do with any regiments. The Barry Boys' Brigade annual reunion was the occasion that he and Colonel Thomas had been sharing.

Boys' Brigade, young man? Well, I suppose it's a bit like the scouts, though, apparently they had to pledge allegiance to God, or something. Pre-dated the scouts, I found out later. Look it up if you want to, I think it's still going.

Turned out that the two of them, and a few others, had been to a little *soireau* round at Major Dodd's house. Used to be quite a big thing apparently, though these days there were a lot fewer of them. half a dozen at most. Class of 1915 or somewhere near that. The years had taken them in lots of different directions, Dodd had spent a lot of time in India, then Ceylon, finally Aden but when he'd been invalided out, he'd come back to Barry and looked up old friends again.

Anyway, they'd all been round, taken a brandy and soda or three while they were toasting the old times. Around half past nine or so, Colonel Thomas had left. There'd been talk of a taxi, but he'd scorned it. Quite capable of walking two miles home, thank you very much. Yes, a little early, but the Major kept early hours. That was all Major Dodd knew.

Of course, we had to do those questions. Enemies? Girlfriends? Bloody Russian spies? Well, what would the poor Major know from the vantage point of his wheelchair? Bugger all, you'd expect, and bugger all it was.

Naturally, I asked him for the names of the other people who'd been at the reunion, since perhaps we should be having a chat with all of them, on the off-chance they'd stabbed the Colonel and dragged him onto the slide. I dunno, maybe they'd harboured a grudge since 1915.

No problem. Dai Wilson, Carwyn Jones, Handel Nicholas, Dai Morgan...and.....what was the name of the last bloke? God, my memory son.........

Ah, yes.

Charlie Bynon.

He, he, he.

Well, sorry son, couldn't resist.

That was a bugger, because I had to break it to the Major that we now had two of his friends lying in the Barry General Mortuary.

He took it very badly, as it happens, son. I never saw a man closer to tears than the Major that day. Old soldier, though. Stiff upper lip and all that, but he was distraught. He'd never married, no relatives left, and his old friends were like family to him. To lose two in two days was a terrible blow. Just terrible.

No, he knew of no reason at all why anyone would want to hurt either of them, much less cold-blooded murder.

I told you we're thorough, son, and try never to believe anything we can't prove, so I gritted my teeth and asked the Major to account for his whereabouts on the nights in question. At first I thought he was going to explode, but he bit his lip and nodded. He usually went to bed early. Blair was a qualified nurse apparently, and used to give him a shot of something to put him out, generally around half past ten. Blair confirmed that the Major had gone to bed around then both nights.

I had to ask though, just because someone sits in a wheelchair and tells you they can't walk a step......

So. it seemed I had quite a few new people to interview. I pulled Lewis off the background checks, and we started on the surviving members of the 1915 Boys' Brigade group. The Major had provided me with addresses, thank God. You don't want to be searching a Welsh phone book for people called Jones and Morgan.

Let's see what I can remember.

Dai Wilson. Retired butcher he was. Little bloke, shook a bit. Parkinson's it could have been. Or the DTs for all I know..

DTs, son *delirio tremolo.* It's what drunks get.

Dreadfully upset to hear about the deaths of his two old friends. You must remember, young man, that an awful lot of people didn't have the TV, and most of them never saw a newspaper, especially the older people. And there was really no connection between the seven of them, apart from the one that went back fifty years, so people weren't likely to run up and tell him.

He knew nothing. He'd left the reunion first, because his wife was a little unwell, and he'd wanted to be back early. Gone straight home to Barry Road. He'd been in all night on the Wednesday when somebody was drowning Bynon. His wife confirmed it. Hardly a cast iron alibi, but I couldn't quite see him dragging two big blokes around. And why would he have wanted to? I'm no judge of acting, but he seemed terribly cut up.

Carwyn Jones was a bus driver, three weeks short of retirement. He was working, according to his wife, so we drove down to Barry Bus Station. Not before making sure that he'd been in by ten on the night of Colonel Thomas' murder, and in all night on the Wednesday.

We had to wait half an hour for him, and it was wasted time really. He'd gone straight home from the reunion, and never left the house on Wednesday night. He'd heard some talk about the two murders, but never connected it to his friends.

Handel Nicholas was a former school teacher at the Barry Grammar and was much more help. Apparently, he and Colonel Thomas lived in pretty much the same direction, so while they were putting on their coats in the Major's hall, they decided to walk part of the way home together and have a nightcap at The Ship, just opposite the Docks. Bugger, just a little outside the area I'd sent the photo round. They'd had one, and then the other half. After that their paths diverged, so they'd said goodnight. He was another one who didn't read the papers, and another one who looked completely stunned by the news.

It didn't look like we were getting too far, but there was still Dai Morgan to go. Or Mr David Parry Morgan, MA LIB as the brass plate outside his office said. Solicitor, son. He was astounded to hear the news too. It seemed no bugger in Barry ever read a newspaper, listened to the radio news or turned on the TV.

Awful business. They'd managed to stay in touch for nearly fifty years, and now this? Dreadful. Major Dodd would be devastated, he'd been so enthusiastic about their meetings, all of them were pretty much the only family he had. His whereabouts? Well, he'd come straight home from the reunion by car on the Tuesday. Wednesday night he'd been at a reception in the Mayor's parlour until nearly midnight.

It wasn't really helping. I asked him a few more questions, then asked him how long Major Dodd had been in his chair. Dunno why. Five or six years he thought. Shame really, all that money and couldn't enjoy it.

Hullo?? All what money?

Oh, didn't I know? His father had been Dodd Foods. Big cereal manufacturer. probably the biggest in Wales. Bought out by Kellogs in the forties. The Major must have inherited a million or so when the old man died. Much good it did him. No family to leave it all to. In fact ....

Bloody Hell.

As simple as that.

Well, it took a while, sonny, because he wasn't going to show it to us without a court order, or the Major's permission, and I was buggered if I was going to let him phone the Major. Lewis went off and found a tame judge to sign the necessary, while I sat in our solicitor friend's office and drank his tea. He wasn't unco-operative once I explained my theory, but he needed to do things by the book.

Maybe it even occurred to him that he might be saving his own life.

And eventually Lewis came back with the paperwork and Thomas showed it to me. No great surprise at all.

Last Will and Testament of Henry Arthur Llewellyn Dodd.

A bloody tontine.

No? Well I wouldn't expect you to, it's not a word that's used much these days. I only knew it from the old Batman comics where it was a common plot. You see everyone thought of Batman as kids' stuff, but he wasn't dubbed the World's Greatest Detective for nothing. I learned an awful lot from him and Sherlock Holmes.

Tontine?

It was originally a French investment system. A bunch of people paid in and received interest. As subscribers died over the years, the survivors copped for the dead people's share. Last man standing got the lot. I think they made it illegal after a while, for pretty obvious reasons. Bloody tempting, eh?

Well the Major had made a tontine will.

Everything of which he stood possessed was to be divided amongst the surviving members of the Barry Boys Brigade 1915 group ... to whit .... well, the people we'd mentioned, and .... one other person.

You've got it son, Corporal Blair.

So, one more question for our solicitor friend.

Who knew?

Well, him of course. He'd never heard the Major mention it at any of the reunions, so he was fairly sure the others didn't. The Major's next door neighbours had been asked to come in and witness his signature, but he was pretty sure they hadn't read the thing.

So, the $64,000 question. Did the Corporal know?

Let's ask him.

We drove back up to Romilly Park road and rang the bell. Corporal Blair let us in and showed us into the lounge. He left to make some tea, and I asked the Major the all important question. Had he ever told the Corporal about his will?

Well, of course he had, loyal servant, needed to know he was taken care of. Owed him everything.

Oh dear, oh dear, oh bloody dear.

Edward Charles Blair, I arrest you for the wilful murders of ..... blah ...blah ... blah ... you are not obliged to say anything, but anything you do say.... etc etc etc.

I was worried about the Major, but he took it fairly well. He had an agency he used to call when Blair took his holidays, so they'd send someone round. I dunno about people, son, but the look he gave Blair, it seemed his heart was broken. All those years of trust, eh?

Well, we sweated Corporal Blair. We could do a little more in those days. We told him we had a couple of witnesses who would swear to having seen him at the Cold Knap lake, and another one who'd seen him taking a pint in The Ship. That was where he cracked.

"But I waited outside The Ship that night".

Poor sod was none too bright,

We had a little crack and we worked at it, son. Kept at him. Eventually he split wide open.

He knew about the will, of course. His share would have kept him in luxury for life, but greed does strange things to people. He decided to shorten the odds. He'd heard the two of them discussing the nightcap at The Ship, so as soon as he'd jabbed the Major, he'd driven down there after them. A fifty-fifty chance which one he picked, so Mr Handel Nicholas owed his life to dumb luck. Though he's long dead now, of course.

Blair followed the Colonel most of the way home, then stabbed him and dragged the body into the playground where it was nice and dark. No witnesses, the playground was in darkness, so he had plenty of time to get himself home, before anyone was likely to discover Colonel Thomas' body. The Major's jab would keep him out till morning.

Bit of a listener at doors was our corporal, so he

knew about the Doctor's regular Wednesday night drink. Same system. Jab his master, then off to Cold Knap. Hang around outside the hotel till closing time. Follow a little way behind. Not too difficult, son, old doctors don't expect people to be following them. Just as Dr. Bynon was passing the lake, he'd coshed him, then dragged him over, held his face underwater. Pushed him out into the middle.

Stupid sod. He'd have copped for over a hundred thousand, a King's ransom back then, so what did he need to get involved in murder for? And besides which, what was the plan? Even if he'd managed to top all the others and we'd never made the connection ..... once the bloody will was read it was all going to be as plain as day.

Just as well for us that most criminals aren't too bright.

The confession was all we had, and a decent barrister might have got him off, but it never came to that. He was on remand in Cardiff Gaol when he hanged himself from the bars with his own trousers. Couple of the warders ended up in trouble over that for not keeping a better eye on him, though nobody had any reason to think he was suicidal.

The Major died two months later ...... heart trouble apparently. Broken heart I reckoned. The four remaining Boys' Brigade members cashed in. They're long since dead now, of course.

I got plenty of kudos for it.

I was at pains to point out the assistance I'd had from DS Lewis, who I felt, was a very efficient policeman indeed, with strong possibilities for promotion. Perhaps he might benefit from a transfer to a larger area?

The Powers That Think They Are took my advice and transferred him to Cardiff. He didn't appear to want to go, but it would surely improve his career prospects. He no doubt got promoted to Inspector in a few more years. I didn't bother following his career.

That WPC Langley would have to find someone else to light her cigarettes for her.

What a shame, eh?

The Graveyard

Do you know, I really haven't thought that much about my early years with the CID for ages, sonny. Barry seems like an awfully long time ago now. Of course, that might be because it is a bloody long time ago, dare say you weren't even born then. No? Thought not.

Hard to describe the sixties to someone who wasn't there. Ten years when the world changed out of all recognition. Lots of things would never be the same again, we were finally getting over the war, young people were starting to be heard from, music was changing. We started the decade in suits, and ended it in jeans.

Quite a nice turn of phrase that, if I do say so myself. Well, yes, I did practise it a bit before I came out. Never been much of a poet.

Oh yes, the biggest difference of all. They invented the Pill too. Bloody best invention ever. Took the worrying out of womanising. (Do me a favour, sonny, leave that bit out, the wife reads The Mail sometimes).

Some things hadn't changed all that much, mind you. Barry Island was still the favourite holiday destination for all the miners from the Valleys. For some of them those two weeks were just about the only sun they ever saw, poor sods. The trains would be packed from Cardiff in June, July and August and all the guest houses did a roaring trade. Lovely people, never any trouble at all with them. Used to come down with the whole family. Grandfather in his flat cap and suit, Grandmother with the blue rinse. Mam and Da and all the kids. Rent a few deckchairs and a windbreak and make a day of it on the beach. Kids would dig a hole and build a castle, then bury Da. Five o'clock, and off for fish and chips.

Of course, most of them couldn't afford anything like two weeks, so they'd come down for the day on the train, or a coach. Suppose I was lucky, I grew up there. It was all free for me sonny, I'd lived there all my life.

Simpler times, my son, simpler times.

For some reason, people from the Midlands were attracted to it like a magnet. You'd have thought Blackpool or Scarborough or somewhere would have been a lot nearer and more popular. But no. Coaches used to come down from Birmingham all the time packed with holidaymakers. Mind you I suppose anywhere's better than bloody Birmingham.

Joke, son, a joke. Never been there. Never wanted to. Odd thing about Birmingham, it's the second largest city in Britain, two million people, yet you almost never meet anyone who comes from there. Never met one when I was in the Met. Maybe it's so wonderful that they never leave. I dunno. I do know that they used to like the Welsh seaside though. Walk along the promenade on a nice summer's day and you'd hear nothing but Brum and Valleys' accents.

Barry was a quiet town in those days, though I'm told it's gone downhill. Suppose the whole country has. Too much bloody immigration if you ask me, all those......well, we'll leave that, shall we? Back to Barry. Nice place. We never had any of the Mods and Rockers violence that broke out in other seaside towns.

No?

Well they were sort of rival gangs, though it was all a bit soft really. The Mods had scooters and dressed smart, the Rockers rode motor bikes and wore leather. In theory they couldn't stand each other, though they probably worked in the same factories in the week. They'd pop down to Margate or wherever and stage "riots" and "running battles", much to the distress of the old ladies, and the horror of the newspapers. I say horror, they loved it of course, big photos of teenagers running about, lurid headlines, more sales. Same as ever, eh sonny? It's all about selling newspapers.

It was mostly all piss and wind, nobody much got hurt, a few bins knocked over, a few windows smashed. The odd broken arm, but nothing serious. Not like the vicious gangs you get these days, guns and all that. But it had pretty much died out by the time I'm talking about.

Yes, well, fair point, I'm not actually talking about it am I? I'm an old man son, I tend to ramble on.

Perhaps a drink might help focus my attention, eh? Make it a brandy, doctor's told me I should cut down on the gin. Hehehe.

Yes, as I say it was a pretty quiet town, and a nice enough little place to live, though, even then I was ambitious to move up to somewhere bigger. Had my eyes fixed on a transfer to The Met. But these things don't happen overnight. Needed to put my time in.

Now, the case we're talking about....or I'm going to talk about when I get round to it....must have happened a year or so after I got made up to Inspector. Detective Inspector, that is, so it would have been in 1964? 1965? I suppose you can check all the dates and names can't you. That Jooggle thing my grandchildren are always going on about. Closed book to me I'm afraid, young man. Wouldn't know how to turn on a computer. In my day they took up a whole room, like those ones on the Science Fiction shows. Used to like that Doctor Who, what was the bloke's name William Troughton?

Sorry, son. Sorry.

Alright, the case.

We called it the Graveyard Murder, though you'd never guess why unless you'd been in Barry back then. Nothing to do with a cemetery really. But then again....

I'll tell you it the way I found out about it, I'm not much

of a story teller, so I'll just stick to the facts and what I know.

I think it was July. Summer for sure, with plenty of visitors down, the funfair and gift shops doing a roaring trade, everybody enjoying themselves and getting sunburnt in a bloody hot summer. Summers always seemed longer and hotter when I was young, and suncream was just for babies or poofs, so you'd see some bloody painful sunburn. The fatter they were, the more they burnt I always thought. Nobody really worried too much about it, they hadn't invented skin cancer then.

Sunday, I am sure of that, because there was a huge cricket match on. Glamorgan versus the International Cavaliers. That was what the BBC used to show on a Sunday afternoon, a quick game between the local county and a lot of famous names. All for charity, and it attracted a huge crowd. Glamorgan never played in Barry, you see. Cardiff or Swansea yes, even bloody Colwyn Bay (though I'm buggered if I know what that's got to do with Glamorgan. Hundred and fifty miles away). I'm almost sure Garry Sobers was there .... but I could be wrong. Most of the uniformed boys were down there on traffic control and policing the crowd. Not that they'd need to do much with a Welsh cricket crowd in those days, so they probably spent all afternoon watching the game, but the Island was pretty much as crowded as it had ever been. Beautiful afternoon all round.

We didn't have much on at the time, as I recall. In

fact I was spending Sunday at home with my mother. Enduring her Sunday lunch cooking. She was a reasonable enough cook, but always had problems with timing. The chicken would be ready by twelve, the vegetables boiled to buggery by half past and the whole lot left to go cold until it was warmed up by thick gravy at one. Still, blood's thicker than water, eh? Her bloody gravy was a damned sight thicker than both, I'll tell you.

What? Well, I'm a bloody policeman, not a lady novelist, son .... just cut out the bits you don't want. Women writers always tell you what people had to eat. Nothing ever happens except at meal times in their books.

Anyway, I was at Mum's when my police radio went off. Body found at the Graveyard. I needed to get down there as soon as possible. Shame they couldn't have found it two hours earlier, or I'd have been spared an afternoon of indigestion. I knew about the cricket, so I told them to send a Police Car over to pick me up. Took about ten minutes. Police Station was in Jenner Road, and Mum lived in Pontypridd Road.

Well, as I said, I'd made Inspector by then, so I rated a proper Squad Car rather than the poxy Ford Anglia. Ford Zephyr this was. Tidy motor. At the time, of course. You boys would sooner use a horse and cart now.

Horse, son...it's a big animal with a leg at each

corner. Used to be popular last century. No, you're right, I'll never make a comedian. How about another one of these, while I collect my thought?

So, come on, let's get the story told, eh?

They picked me up and turned on the bell. No, it really was a bell in those days, just like a telephone, and we cut through the traffic, out of the town, across the causeway and onto the Island. Ten minutes, quarter of an hour. Could have done it faster if we'd really needed to, but apparently there was no real urgency. The Main Attraction wasn't going anywhere. Drove me down to the Graveyard.

Well, I suppose I really should tell you about The Graveyard.

The early sixties. Those were the days when British Rail, as it used to be called, was changing over from the lovely old steam engines to diesel or electric or whatever. Yes, I'm old enough to remember steam trains. Just after they invented the wheel, young man. So, they had an awful lot of steam engines they were never going to need again, and they started selling them off for scrap. Well, strange as it may sound, hundreds and hundreds of them got bought by a scrap metal firm in Barry....what were they called ..... Woodyards? Woodfulls? Woodhams? Maybe you can look that up too. They were one of the few firms in Britain who knew how to scrap a steam engine. There was some sort of special technique to it.

I don't bloody know, I was a policeman, not a scrap metal merchant.

Except they never quite got round to scrapping most of the engines, because they also bought a load of wagons, and it was much faster and easier to scrap those first. So, anyone going to Barry Island in the sixties and seventies could have seen hundreds of these old dead giants lined up in sidings, beginning to rust away. No joke, son. Two or three hundred. Graveyard of Steam, it was. Barry was famous for it.

And that's where it started.

Well, we arrived and somebody had been rather efficient, found the bloke with the key and he'd opened the main gate so we could drive straight in. Not that it was the most secure place in the world at the best of times. Plenty of holes in the fence where anyone could walk in and out with no trouble at all. Well, it wasn't as if any bugger was likely to walk out with a fifty ton steam engine under his arm, was it? No, son, I don't know if that's what they really weigh, ask a bloody expert. I do know that I wouldn't have wanted one parked on my foot for very long. And if I planned to steal one, I'd need a bloody big van to take it away in.

We stopped just inside the gate, next to the first engine while the driver got out to see what was what. Huge thing, towering over us. You didn't really appreciate how big they were when you saw them in the station, since you were standing on a three-foot platform. A dead monster now, of course. At that time they hadn't been there all that long, so it was still in fairly good nick. Still had the name plate. "Pride Of Mansfield", I remember it well. On the front buffer someone had scrawled 2/10 in chalk, which I supposed must have been the date it arrived. Or maybe the date it was due to be scrapped. I'm not much of a hand at descriptions and feelings, but it was quite moving to be stood next to something I'd grown up with that was now just a heap of unwanted metal. Made me realise how much the world was changing. Though I'm not sure if that's what I'm thinking now, or what I really felt then. You're always wiser looking back eh, young man?

Constable got back in, we drove on and almost straight away I could see where the commotion was. About halfway down the second siding, there was an ambulance, two more police cars (Ford Anglias this time, horrible looking things) and a couple of other cars. We parked up next to them, and I got out. My sergeant was already there. Good man. What was his name? DS Lloyd? No, no DS Llewellyn. I knew it was something Welsh. Youngish bloke then, shock of jet-black Welsh hair. Smallish, like a lot of Welsh people. Probably just made the minimum height.

Eh? Yes, five foot eight minimum. Five foot four for women I think. Abolished now of course, unfair to ethnic minors. Happy, Dopey and Doc could probably get in these days. Especially if they were minors. (Yes, alright, cut out what you like).

Anyhow, Dai Llewellyn's there. I need to know all about it, and he's the man to tell me. So he does.

Couple of kids apparently, coming out here to look at the engines and do some spotting. Trainspotting, son. You get a little book and you write down all the numbers of the trains that you've seen. Normally you do it at stations, but this place you could do hundreds at once.

Was it a film? Never heard of it, don't go to the cinema much. Must have been a bloody dull film, watching people with bobble hats and notebooks writing down numbers.

Buggered if I ever saw the attraction, but it takes all sorts and there's plenty of hobbies that I don't understand. Used to be kids who'd go bus-spotting. Write down the numbers of all the buses they'd been on. Especially the Cardiff trolleybuses.

Trolleybuses? Ah, it doesn't matter, It's all a long time ago. Let's try to stick to the story, shall we?

Where was I?

Yes. Couple of kids, trainspotting. Shouldn't have been in there by rights, but not doing any harm. Well, of course, as any kid would, they'd write down the number, then jump up onto the footplate and pretend they were Casey Jones (look it up son, look it up). Pure dumb luck that after half an hour or so, they climbed into one and found her. Shit scared, ran like buggery for the nearest phone box and dialled 999, just like their mums had taught them. Waited by the phone box for the first police car and then showed the boys in blue what they'd found.

They were still there. Couple of kids of twelve or thirteen. I managed to detect that they probably weren't the guilty parties. These days, I dare say I wouldn't be so sure, the way things are going. Anyway, I got them taken home by a WPC. Gave them ten bob each out of my own pocket, for doing the right thing.

Alright, fifty pence. Fairly decent sum of money for a kid then, but they deserved it. Could have just run away and left us none the wiser. People were a little more public spirited in the sixties, kids used to think of the Police as their friends, rather than their target.

No, don't remember their names. Probably grandfathers now. Might be in the file, though I doubt the South Wales Police will be letting you look at it.

Freedom Of Information Act? Never heard of it, young man. Sounds a bloody stupid idea to me. Busybodies' Charter more like.

Let's get on.

A body, of course. They'd left her up in the engine, "Sir Richard Greville" it was called. No idea who he was. I had to climb up to take a look. Nasty, but then they usually are. There's rarely anything pretty about a violent death, young man. I can't really remember what I saw and what I was told, so I'll just give you the facts. Twenty-five to thirty, blonde, but not natural. Healthy enough girl (well, apart from being dead), nicely built, must have been quite pretty, Wearing a floral print dress with a Littlewoods label (we've talked about catalogues, I think) and a red cotton scarf around the neck, worn rather too tightly to permit continued breathing.

Strangled yes, son.

Who was she?

No ideas. No handbag, so no possibilities of identification, unless she'd thought to sew name-tapes into her clothes, which, amazingly enough, she hadn't. None of the boys and girls recognised her, though a strangling rarely leaves a girl looking her best.

Flippant? Maybe son, but you didn't see her .... or any of the hundreds of others I've seen in my time. Maybe a little black humour helps. Doctors always used to be fairly flippant too, but then they probably saw a lot more corpses than I ever did.

I was a Detective Inspector, so I did some detecting. First thing I was able to detect was that she'd most likely been killed where she lay. Nobody in their right mind would drag a dead body halfway down a row of engines, then haul it up six feet.

Right mind? Yes, well, fair point. But even a nutter would have needed to be Superman to carry a dead nine stone woman that far and then haul her up onto the engine. Of course, there could have been more than one of them ...... but I didn't quite see it that way at the time.

I took a good look at the body. It wasn't something I relish, but it was the job. I'm no Sherlock Holmes, but I did my best. Couldn't find any calluses on the hands to speak of a career in typewriting, bunions on the feet to tell me she was a ballet dancer. To my eyes, nothing useful. Police Doctor said she'd been dead at least four days. Thank God it hadn't been more or she'd have been stinking to high heaven in that heat. As it was, you were unlikely to be able to tell what perfume she'd been wearing.

No, I'm not unfeeling, son, it's just the way things are. I've said before that if you saw them all as people, you'd be in a lunatic asylum inside five years. She was a case, a dead body, not a young woman who'd been savagely murdered. You had to divorce yourself from it as much as you can.

Yes, a drink or two does help, now that you mention it. Same again. Funny, I never used to drink at all until I joined the CID. Never yet met a teetotal detective.

Well, we'd seen as much as we could hope to, and it was time to hand things over to the professionals.

Madam was loaded into the ambulance and driven away to Barry General. Meanwhile the fingerprint boys wanted to know what to do. Well, be serious, who the bloody hell could manage to fingerprint an entire steam engine. Not enough talcum powder in the world. I told them to try the ladder and the cab, but there were probably thousands. And a fingerprint's only any use if you have some fingers to compare it with. Not great surfaces to get prints from either. Still, we tried.

There was nothing much else for me to do. There were no witnesses apart from the kiddies who'd found her and I'd already detected that they probably hadn't strangled a grown woman, lugged her up into a steam engine, waited four days and then called the Law. All we had was a corpse and a lot of work ahead.

For some reason, even then, I had a bad feeling that we wouldn't be solving this one.

Anyway, it was Sunday and, as I said, there really wasn't much more detecting to be done, so I wandered over and watched the cricket for an hour or so. Things like that very rarely happened in Barry, so why not? A warrant card was as good as a ticket. No, turns out Sobers wasn't there now, I remember, but there was a famous England batsman playing. Edrich. John Edrich, Tidy left-hander. Made 92 I think. Glamorgan lost, but it was only a charity game. Funny how you remember some things, but not others. It'll happen to you son. We all get there.

After the cricket finished I wandered off back to Barry and had a few drinks with a young lady of my acquaintance. What was her name.... Elaine .... Elaine Taylor .... no Tyler. Nice girl, I'd been at Primary School with her, but she'd filled out nicely since those days.

None of your damned business, and leave her name out of it anyway. I'm a married man. She's probably on her third marriage by now. Always a bit flighty was Elaine.

So, we come on to Monday, and there's an awful lot of work to do. Sadly no country house with eight idiosympathic suspects to grill, just a dreadful load of routine enquiries. That's real policing for you sonny, very little glamour and a great deal of shoe leather. Fortunately Detective Inspectors don't need to wear out their own shoes, they have people to do that for them.

The Barry CID wasn't exactly bursting with manpower, so I put in a request for extra, and they sent over a couple of constables from Cadoxton. It still wasn't exactly a task force, but we did what we could.

First priority, of course, was to identify the dear departed. One constable to go through Missing Persons, another to get some posters made and put up in Post Offices, an appeal in the *Barry And District News*. If she was local, we'd be bound to hear something soon. Two more constables to take a photograph round all the hotels, guest houses, caravan parks and so on to see if anyone was missing a guest. We'd managed to get a photograph taken and touched up a bit to make her look a little bit less ..... dead.

One more constable to take a photo round the pubs and the ships at the Docks, just in case Madame was...er....well known to the sailing profession.

Yes, you put it how you like, son. I mean a prozzie. Such ladies do exist, and sadly, the death rate amongst them is higher than their ..... er .... less .... more .... chaste sisters. And where you'll find seafarers, you'll find ladies offering their charms for sale. Or for sail maybe! Hahaha.

Yes, yes, "Worker in the sex industry", whatever you like, young man. When I was in the job PC stood for Police Constable, and that was all. No. I'm not criticising them sonny, people end up in all kinds of places, and it isn't always of their own choosing. Not sure whether that's DI Williams talking in 1966 or ex-Chief Superintendent Williams talking now. We learn as we go along, eh? Even a dinosaur like me has changed his attitudes a bit in the last forty years.

Anyway, off they went to work.

Me, I sat in my office, sucked a few Spangles (sweeties, son), sorted out some paperwork on a few recent cases and waited for some reports to come in. In all the books, they concentrate on one case at a time, but they tend to overlap in real life, so I had reports to write, forms to fill in and the prospect of a day or two in court to prepare for.

Funnily enough, the first thing to come through was the post-mortem report. Rather quicker than usual. Maybe it was a little more straightforward. Maybe they weren't too busy. I didn't ask.

A woman (I'd spotted that myself, without benefit of medical degree). Age twenty-five to thirty. Death from strangulation (I believe they used some more technical terms, but it doesn't matter). Almost certainly with the scarf that was tied round her neck. Dead approximately four days. No scars, tattoos (well, a woman with tattoos in the sixties would have been one in a million, they're bloody covered in the things these days. Silly bitches.) or birthmarks. Had given birth at least once, and judging by this and that, possibly had an abortion too. Well, it was the sixties, son. You couldn't just show up and ask for one, it was an underground thing. Usually did some damage I'm told, though I was never keen to find out the gory details. "This and that" will do for me. Some bruising on her upper arms, but there was no evidence of sexual assault, or indeed recent sexual activity.

Food for thought, and I suppose we could draw some conclusions about the type of woman we were dealing with. Probably not the local vicar's wife.

Yes, I know, I'm a neanderthal, mustn't jump to conclusions and all that. And no, we didn't ask any of the local vicars if they were missing a wife. Possibly we missed a trick there.

Anyway, it was more information, but it really didn't get us any nearer identifying the poor girl, much less give us any clues to the bastard who'd done it. But surely somebody would miss a daughter, sister, work colleague, wife, girlfriend?

It seemed not.

Days went past and we heard nothing, until the

Friday. Well, that was our best hope, because the *Barry And District* came out on a Thursday afternoon. So Friday it was.

I was in my office at Jenner Road around tennish when the desk sergeant came in. Linane I think his name was. Apparently there was a Mrs Nicholas at the front desk, who thought she might know the dead girl. Owned a guest house. I told him to bring the lady in, and organise some tea and biscuits. Digestives I'm afraid, but then I was only an Inspector.

Yes, I'm sure of the name, Nicholas, same as my middle name, so it struck a chord. In she came. I dunno, fifty or so. Tight lipped. Thin. Looked like a guest house owner. I offered her some tea and biscuits and we got to the point.

She had a Guest House on Porthkerry Road. Respectable place, she assured me. Who was I to argue? "Skibbereen" it was called. Her grandfather had been Irish, so she'd chosen an Irish name for it. I may have looked as if I was losing interest, bit like you now, sonny, because she suddenly got to the point.

One of her guests for the last few months was a young lady from Merthyr, Jean Rodriguez. (No, not necessarily son, there was a lot of Italian and Spanish immigration into Wales after the war). Nice quiet girl she seemed, always paid the rent on time, but Mrs Nicholas hadn't seen her for over a week now, and when she saw the photo in the paper, well, it looked just like her, and she said to Mrs Sykes next door.......

So, you get the picture. and I sent her off to the Barry General mortuary with a WPC. Nice young girl, I remember. Dark hair. Nice enough figure, as far as you could judge from a WPC's uniform. Well, they weren't exactly designed by Mary Quant.

Look her up, son, look her up. Mary Quant, not the WPC.

They were back inside the hour, and Mrs Nicholas was a hundred percent sure that the dead lady was her ex-lodger. Jean Rodriguez from Merthyr.

Naturally, we had quite a few questions for Mrs Nicholas. She was sure it was Merthyr, because Miss Rodriguez had mentioned it to her and to several of the other girls. She'd come down to work at one of the restaurants on the Island for the summer season. No, she didn't mention which one, as far as she could remember. Nice girl she seemed. Kept herself to herself and didn't seem to socialise with any of the other lodgers, but then maybe that was because she never got in until quite late most nights. Probably working a late shift, thought Mrs Nicholas. All the girls had their own keys. She hadn't seen the dead girl since the previous Wednesday.

I asked about boyfriends, and Mrs N. did the predictable indignant bit. No, of course not, she runs a respectable establishment. Gentlemen callers are not permitted in rooms. And nobody had ever come to call for Jean Rodriguez. I promised Mrs Nicholas that we'd get in touch with the girl's next of kin as quickly as possible, because she was making noises about clearing out her clothes so she could let the room again. Well, yes, maybe a little lacking in compassion, but I suppose she had a business to run and bills to pay.

Before that, of course, I needed to take a look at the deceased's room, so I took DS Llewellyn and that same smart young WPC and we drove the landlady back to "Skibbereen".

Looked Victorian to me, not that I'm an architect. Big place on three floors. Six bedrooms and a couple of bathrooms upstairs. Residents' lounge and dining room downstairs. Kitchen of course. Mrs Nicholas had her own self-contained flat in an annexe on the side. Apparently residents got breakfast, which Jean Rodriguez rarely got up for, and evening meal, which she was generally too late for. Probably they fed her at the restaurant, or so Mrs Nicholas thought.

The dead girl's room was on the top floor, so that's where we headed. I've seen bigger rooms, but it was no shoebox. She'd left it very tidy. It had the normal sort of sixties furniture. Granny furniture, I call it. Bed, wardrobe, chest of drawers, dressing table and chair, and an armchair. Decent quality, not like the make-it-yourself stuff they sell you these days. Can't remember what colour the room was painted. I can't remember what colour my own bedroom is painted these days. Probably some cheap prints on the wall, but who cares? Her bedroom, not mine, sonny, keep up.

We went through everything. Nice enough collection of clothes in the drawers and wardrobes. Some decent shoes, not top notch, but not cheap either (We had the WPC to thank for that information). The bottom two drawers were a bit of an eye-opener, as that's where the lady kept her lingerings.

Underwear, son. Yes, that's what I said.

It was racy stuff right enough, in an impressive collection of colours. Quite a few packets of expensive nylons too. The WPC was turning green with envy at the quality of it, and the two of us were open mouthed. Never seen anything like it outside the pages of Parade.

Parade? It was the nearest the sixties got to a naughty magazine sonny. No doubt you'd find it exceedingly tame. Demeaning to women? Probably, but these were primitive times son, we'd barely crawled out of caves and learned to make fire, and we had no Harriet Hatchetface to show us all the error of our ways. Thank God for progress, I say. Parade's long since gone, and we're lucky enough to have a whole internet awash with kiddy porn. Much better, eh?

Back to the frilly flimsies. Of course, you might say that I was jumping to conclusions, but in my experience this wasn't the sort of stuff that the average waitress would wear or could afford. Specialist stuff, you might say.

Never you bloody mind what experience! Cheeky young sweep.

That was the highlight of the search I'm afraid. There was a decent enough collection of ladies' lotions and potions on the dressing table. Again that young WPC told us they were decent quality stuff, but wouldn't cost a fortune. Brushes, nail kit, all the normal stuff apparently. No compact or lipstick, they were no doubt in the handbag, which I felt we were never going to find.

Nothing personal at all. Not a photo, book, library card, letter, diary, bank book, passport, driving licence, wages slip. Nothing to show who she was or what she did or who her family might be. So she was just Jean Rodriguez from Merthyr.

We did all the normal routine stuff and talked to the other girls who lodged there. Couple of wages clerks, a bank clerk, girl who worked in a shop. Can't remember the names of most of them and it doesn't matter. They'd hardly ever seen the dead girl, though she'd always seemed pleasant enough. She generally slept late and worked long hours, so it was hardly surprising. No callers, never saw a letter for her.

The only one who was any help at all was a plain little thing who taught in Romilly Juniors.....what was her name....Edith Roberts or Robinson. Dark hair she had, a little older than the rest, might have been thirty. Glasses. She'd been a little bit friendlier with Miss Rodriguez, they'd even gone to the cinema together one Saturday afternoon. Some Beatles film at the old Tivoli, not that it matters. She said Jean was a bright friendly girl, but didn't seem to talk much about family or friends. Never heard her mention a boyfriend or husband, despite doing a little gentle pumping. They mostly talked about clothes shops. She thought it was Forte's restaurant that she worked in.

It seemed that would be all we could get from "Skibbereen". Didn't really seem to be much point in fingerprinting the room, since we were pretty sure she'd never had any callers, and very sure she hadn't died there. I told Mrs Nicholas she could put the clothes and toiletries into her box room until the next-of-kin could be contacted, which should be very soon now.

Back to the station.

I sent a constable down to the Island with the dead girl's photo and told him to find out which restaurant had employed her. I got the WPC .... what was her name...Jane, Jane Langdon (amazing how stuff comes back to you) to put in a call to the Merthyr Police and get them to trace the dead girl's family. Another nasty little job for someone, breaking the news, but once again it wouldn't be me. Then I went home, it had been a long day.

Do you know son, I won't. I really think it's time I was getting home to the wife. This one seems to be taking rather a long time to tell, maybe I am rambling on too much. Still, gives you time to get started on typing it up eh? Assuming you remembered to put a tape in that thing? No, I do know what "digital" means, young man ..... I'm not a complete dinosaur. What say we try to finish this one next week? Tuesday? Suits me.

No, this is fine, quiet enough little club. Well, yes, my place might be even quieter, but they do a nicer class of brandy here, and the wife isn't watching. She gets a little concerned about my health these days. Dunno why, I've been a drinker all my life, and it's never done me any harm. Apart from the blood pressure. And the diabetes. Spot of gout. Angina. Other than that, I'm right as rain.

I'll see you then.

Well, here we are again then. No, don't mind if I do. Make it a large one if you would, and a good splash of tonic. We've still got a bit of a way to go on the Graveyard Case and I wouldn't want to get too dry. No, nothing to eat, I had a nice lunch over the road. Steak and Kidney pudding.

Well, I don't really care how much fat and carbohydrate is in it, young man, it's my stomach and I like to feel it full.

Course, there was a lot less of it in those days, though I think I'd stopped playing Rugby by then. Glamorgan Police used to have a bloody good side back then. Wing three-quarter. Had a couple of trials for Cardiff, but I really needed to concentrate on the career. And maybe I was just a little too slow for the top level. Plus, I needed to make a living, and rugby was all amateur then. Allegedly.

Well, I dare say it isn't all that interesting to your readers, so let's get back to the case. Where was I? Oh, that's impressive, typed out already. Let me see .... So, we'd got as far as the Friday after we found the body. Let me think.

Yes, I sloped off home, had some tea and then met up with a young lady and took her to the pictures. Karen Jones, I remember, but again you won't be needing to use the name. Nice girl, very friendly indeed. Very friendly. Well, I was a single man, had my own flat in Romilly Road. No, I didn't live with my mother, thank you very much. Some day I'll tell you more about my mother. Hallowe'en might be a good time.

So much for Friday.

Don't get too many days off when there's a murder to be sorted out, so I was back down the station at sparrowfart on Saturday, to see what developments there'd been. Or rather not been as it turned out.

The constable we'd sent down to the Island had drawn a complete blank in every restaurant, chip shop, café and hotel down there. Nobody recognised the dead girl and nobody was missing a waitress. Fair play to the man, he used his brain and took it round all the places in town too, with exactly the same lack of result.

I wasn't exactly bowled over with surprise. Those late hours, that flash underwear and some of the details in the post-mortem had left me thinking that perhaps this young lady hadn't been making her living dishing out steak and ice-cream to the tourist crowd. Perhaps I was stereostyling, son, but I've always found that the most obvious explanation is usually the right one. If it walks like a duck and quacks, as they say.....

Well, then it probably is a duck. Never heard that one? Bloody hell.

I had my own theory about Miss Rodriguez's occupation, and needed to get some confirmation from one or two people. The people in question surely would not be up and about at that time on a Saturday morning, so that was a little job for later. Thought I might do that one myself, rather than overburden the minions. Still, we were nothing if not thorough, so I sent the same poor constable over to Cold Knap and Penarth with her photo, just on the off-chance. I'll save you the suspense. Nothing of any interest.

The next fly in the woodpile arrived around lunchtime, when they put a call through to me from Inspector Edmonds at Merthyr. Decent enough bloke, another ex-Rugby man. Second row, not that it matters.

Well, maybe it didn't hurt either of our careers, but what of it, eh?

Apparently they'd been through the phone book up there and then the electoral roll. Rodriguez wasn't all that unusual a name, but it wasn't Jones or even Williams, so there weren't all that many. And none of them was missing a Jean. Or indeed any young lady of any name. They'd tried all the surrounding area too, and actually found one Jean Rodriguez, but she was a mother of two, forty years old and very much alive. None of the families, apart from hers, had ever heard of a Jean Rodriguez, or had any young lady relatives unaccounted for,

Bugger.

It seemed that we were back to square one. No suspects, no witnesses, no motive and now no bloody victim. Could things get worse?

Of course they could.

The phone rang again.

The Super wanted to see me.

Superintendent Henry Watkins. Number one at Barry Nick. A name to make strong men quiver, the Stalin of South Wales, the Genghis Khan of Glamorgan.

Nah, not really son. I know, it's what you're expecting isn't it? Every Detective Inspector is meant to have a Superintendent who never lets up on them. Makes their lives a misery. Frost, Morse, they solve every case brilliantly, yet still the Super despises them, won't trust them and chews them out every five minutes. Until finally they get the result, and it's "Well done, Inspector."

And then, of course, next episode, it's back to daggers drawn.

More bollocks.

Watkins was a damned good policeman, helped me every step of the way and supported me in everything I did. We worked together and made a damned good team. Understandably, he liked to keep his finger on the pulse, and that was what he was doing now.

I went along to his office. I saw him look down and guessed he was thinking about offering me a drink from the bottle we both knew he kept in the bottom drawer. A little early in the day, so he offered me tea instead. Another constable brought it. Biscuits too. Bourbon Creams. Posh. Well, he was the Super after all.

What was he like? Big bloke, thinning hair. Horn

rimmed glasses. Grey suit ... or dark blue. What can I say? He looked like a senior policeman. Long dead of course, must have been nearly sixty then.

Well then, he wanted to know what progress was being made in the Rodriguez case. He might not have called it that. He might have used the words "Dead trollop on the steam engine," it's a long time ago, my memory isn't what it was.

I was obliged to confess that any progress I thought I'd made had been wiped out by the news that morning, but there were a couple of lines of enquiry which I felt might be worth pursuing.

He listened. He nodded at the first one.

Then I got on to number two, which I knew was going to be a more difficult one to sell.

He winced. He thought. Finally he nodded.

"It's not going to be popular with the boys and girls on a Sunday, Williams but you're right, it has to be done. I'll sanction the overtime."

Decent old sod, Henry Watkins. I've met plenty of arsehole Superintendents since, but that's another story. Maybe several.

Bugger me, my throat's dry. Another one of these would be good.

Bit less tonic this time.

As I recall, I broke the news to them all straight away, There was a lot of muttering, but then they started thinking about the overtime and the muttering died down a little. The old Filthy Luger always helps, eh?

Now we had a few more things to sort out. So far, I'd managed to keep the story pretty local. It had just been a "Woman found dead" thing, but now we needed some help from the bigger boys. I made some calls to the crime desks of the Western Mail and the South Wales Echo. Gave them the story. "Unidentified woman found strangled, do you know this person?" I still didn't tell them exactly where, I didn't want The Graveyard turning into a magnet for nutters. They both sent a motorcycle round for a copy of the photo, and promised to splash it all over the next edition.

Maybe I should have given them the story sooner, but I felt the next of kin deserved to be told first. Anyway, in those days we had quite a good relationship with the Crime Editors and we did each other favours. They'd hold off on a story if we asked them too, in exchange for a scoop later.

You play ball with me and I'll scratch yours.

Yes, I'm bloody sure it is different these days, son. I'm just glad to be out of it.

While all that was happening, I sent a couple of PCs back up to "Skibbereen" to have another chat with the ladies there. You know, were they sure she'd said

Merthyr? Might it not have been Monmouth, Macynllyth, Manchester, bloody Madagascar for all I know. They came back with nothing, of course, but we had to try every possibility. And everyone was sure it was Jean Rodriguez. Not Jane or Joan or bloody Blodwyn Jones.

You see, in those days, people didn't demand identification every time you wanted to have a piss. Three quarters of the population would have had no identification anyway. People didn't tend to go abroad, less than half the population had a driving licence, ration cards had been abolished fifteen years before, so what were people meant to use? Bloody library card? If someone showed up at a guest house and told you she was Jean Rodriguez from Merthyr, you'd just believe her.

And you'd have been wrong as it turned out.

For the moment I'd done all I could at the Station, and I had a night's work ahead of me, so I'd be needing something to eat. I wasn't in the mood for the canteen, so I drove down to the Island. I took my own car this time. Vauxhall Viva, dark blue. I never liked to look too conspicuous. No Jaguars or anything. Not on my pay, that's for sure. Went to Fortés and indulged myself in the full cod, chips, peas, bread and butter and cup of tea. Followed by ice-cream. Probably about three shillings all in. Fifteen pence in your money. They hadn't invented cholesterol in those days.

Then I went across to The White Hart for a pint or two.

They hadn't invented breathalysers either!

Around nineish I decided it was time to look for a little information. There were one or two specific informants I had in mind, but anyone of half a dozen others might have been able to help too. It was a nice warm summer night, and still light, so I tried the promenade first. Walked up and down a few times, and was just about to give up, when I spotted one of my first choices. She wasn't looking my way, so I was able to take her arm almost before she saw me.

"Evening, Jenny. How's business?"

I'm pretty sure that Madame wasn't any too pleased to see me, but she gave me a lovely smile. There might have been a tone of sarcasm in the greeting.

"Mr. Williams. How lovely to see you. Are you looking for a little company this evening? On the house?"

Saucy little minx. When I'd known Jenny James at school she'd been pretty damned flirtatious, but it had never gone anywhere. It certainly wasn't going to now that I was a DI. Trust me, son, I've seen a lot of good careers thrown away like that.

No, no. Figure of speech. Can't think of any examples at the moment. None at all.

I point out that I'm not looking for any company, however delightful, nor am I looking to increase my arrest statistics just at the moment. Her smile became even warmer. What I needed was a little information.

I showed her the photograph.

She nodded.

"Anna. Nice girl. New. Well, this isn't London Mr. Williams, and there's plenty of custom to go around, especially when the boats come in and the coaches come down. We're not too protective of our little patch. Most of us try to look out for each other."

She went quiet then, seemed to think for a minute or two.

"She's dead, isn't she?"

She didn't need my nod. I wouldn't have been showing the photograph if the girl had been caught shoplifting.

"Shame, she was a nice girl. Catch the bastard for us, David."

I had a few more questions, but she had little in the way of answers. Anna was from Pontypridd and happy to gossip, but she never gave much away about herself. Not even her surname. Jenny had no idea about her clientele, though like most of her .... colleagues, she worked the promenade and the dock pubs as well.

I decided to try a couple of dock pubs too, told her to be careful, and was all for walking away, but she dug her fingers into my arm hard.

"Catch the bastard for us David. Please."

What could I say? What would you have said?

I drove down to the Docks and headed for the nearest pub. What was it called? I dunno. Does it matter? Call it the Prince Of Wales.
Another pint and a good look round. At the other end of the bar sat another familiar face. Well, I suppose a face can't sit, but you know what I mean, don't you? I wandered down towards her. There was a sailor chatting to her, but he looked at me and moved away. Maybe the size, maybe I just looked like a policeman. I tend to.

"Evening Sue. How's tricks?"

Again the warm smile. Again it wasn't quite convincing.

"Mr Williams, how nice to see you. On your own?"

Couldn't be bothered with the banter any more so I just showed her the photo. Anna from Ponty, right enough. Nice girl, but somebody'd done her hadn't they?

Another nod from me.

No useful answers from her either. Sue knew nothing about Anna's clients, be they regular or occasional.

She'd seen her with blokes in suits, sunburnt fat men, sailors. All sorts. Promenade and dock pubs too.

Odd thing though. She used almost the same phrase.

"You'll catch the bastard David. Catch him for us."

I'd had enough and drove home to my flat. I seem to remember having quite a few whiskies before going to bed.

I prefer gin these days, sonny, if you're going.

Sunday morning, bright and early. Don't think I was feeling too chipper really, but I had work to do and I'd never let a hangover stop me yet. Still haven't come to that.

I dropped in at the station and suggested to one of the constables that he might try a phone call to the Pontypridd police, and ask them if there were any Anna Rodriguezes missing. Or anyone at all. It seemed a pretty forlorn hope, but you have to dot the Ts and cross the Is, eh?

Then it was off to the main business of the day. Something I should have done a week earlier if I'd had half a brain. Decent of the Super not to have pointed it out.

Search the bloody Graveyard.

By the time I got down there, there were twenty officers and DS Llewellyn waiting about. Most of them were probably dying for a smoke, but it wouldn't have looked good in uniform. Especially since the Press had got wind of it and there were a couple of reporters and cameramen around. They were smoking themselves sick of course.

I had a word with the gentlemen of the Press first. Told them to stay outside the fence, but I'd share anything we found straight away. Who knows, we might need their help.

Then I talked to the boys and girls.

We were looking for anything out of the ordinary. In engines, under engines, beside the tracks, in any outbuildings. If they could find a woman's handbag I'd be delighted, but I was pretty sure there was no chance of that. They'd been told to bring sandwiches, it could be a very long day indeed.

Maybe I haven't described the Graveyard properly to you, young man. It was huge. It was basically a railway siding, or marshalling yard or whatever. Disused of course. Six or seven parallel tracks, all of them crammed full of dead steam locomotives. Three hundred or so, I think. For each one the boys and girls would need to climb up the ladder to the footplate, check the cab, open the firebox, crawl inside and shine the torches about. On both sides of the tracks there were acres of rough ground, long grass, sand dunes. It was a nightmare place to try to search, and I doubted we'd be leaving before dusk.

It took three hours.

I heard a shout away to my left, over in one of the patches where the grass was the longest. I put down the News Of The World, got out of the car and ran over. Constable Perkins it was who'd found it, and proved me right a week later than should have happened.

The man, or what was left of him, was lying face down in the long grass, where he couldn't be seen until you were almost on top of him. Grey suit, brown hair was all I could really tell you from a first viewing, and the smell discouraged me from getting much closer. I sent Perkins back to the squad car to radio for the ambulance and the Police Surgeon. I let the search continue until they arrived, then I sent most of them home.

What?

Well, yes, I could have kept them at it, but I'd found what I had a feeling I might find.

The handbag? I doubt it. Maybe it's still out there somewhere, but I don't think so, and I wouldn't have thought it would tell us anything useful now. Probably went into a litter bin the night she died.

So, there we were again at the Graveyard, with a dead body and the Police Surgeon. McGill ..... it just came back to me. Dr. McGill. The things you can remember when you're not trying, eh?

Rather him than me, for sure, as the poor sod had been lying out in the sun for ten days or so, and wasn't smelling any too sweet. Not strangled this time. Stabbed. Stabbed in the back, probably punctured a kidney, so he'd have bled to death pretty quickly apparently. Couple of minutes at most.

Now that we were there looking at it, it seemed as if he might have been running through the grass away from the engines, though the grass had had chance to spring up again. There were drops of blood here and there, in a line from the engine where we'd found the girl to where he was lying. Just the odd drop, mind you, son. The doctor reckoned that most of the bleeding would have been internal or soaked up by the suit. For sure, there was a huge black stain on the back of his jacket.

You can call me squeamish, young man, but I've never been much of a watcher for the nasty stuff, so I told Llewellyn to check him for identification, and headed back to the car. I sat there for five minutes or so, staring at the same big old dead giant I'd seen the first time. "The Pride Of Mansfield". I'm not fond of corpses, and it took my mind off it to think of those tons of steel thundering across Nottinghamshire, bound for who knows where, pulling hundreds of people along behind. There just is something romantic about steam trains. Brings out the boy in all of us. Well, maybe not you, then, but you never grew up with them. Trust me, the 4.15 from Waterloo to Tunbridge Wells just isn't the same.

They'd changed the date on the buffer I noticed. 5/12 it read now. I suppose that gave the old beauty an extra couple of months to stand there. Sad to think of all these titans of the railways ending up as school railings and bloody garden gates.

Romantic? Me son? My arse!

There's just something about trains, as I said. No, never had a train set myself, I was growing up during a war, and there wasn't money for things like that.

Bought my grandson a bloody nice one last Christmas though. Funny, he never really took much interest in it at all. According to his mother he spends most of his time playing with his Wee, which doesn't sound too healthy for a growing lad. *O tempura, O morons* as my old Latin teacher used to say.

Anyway, Llewellyn came back to the car.

We're buggered again. No sign of a wallet, driving licence or anything else to identify the dear departed. Jesus, it should be bloody compulsory to sew your name and address into all your clothes. So, if you're counting sonny, that makes two unidentified murder victims in the Barry Island Graveyard, and DI Williams without a single lead.

Yes, I will have another one.

Monday morning it all hit the Press big time. I can remember the headlines in the Western Mail. "Unidentified Man and Prostitute Murdered Amongst Steam Engines."

Always used to find that odd. He was a man, some poor unidentified bloke, but she wasn't allowed the dignity of womanhood. She was a "Prostitute," something a bit lower down the evolutionary scale. As if she mattered much less. Just some cheap tuppeny trollop, no better than she should be, pretty much deserved it.

Sorry, son. It's the gin. Makes me maudlin. Better be something else next time, but I'll finish this one. I'll try to keep off the metaphorics.

We'd still had very little response to the photograph of the girl, and we had none at all to the artist's impression of the bloke. His face was in no condition to be photographed really, ten days of snails, maggots and possibly the odd fox or feral cat does very little for anyone's beauty.

I'd asked Dr. McGill to try and do the post mortem as quickly as possible, just in the vain hope that it would give me something to go on, and he was able to give me some preliminary stuff that afternoon. As he'd guessed at the scene, the deceased had been stabbed in the back, but twice apparently. Long, sharp, narrow-bladed knife. Puncturing his kidney and liver.....or spleen, I don't remember. He'd managed to run fifty yards or so but collapsed and bled to death pretty damned quickly. Bloody nasty.

Five feet eleven, probably aged thirty-five or so, running to fat just a little and some sunburn that must have been pretty painful at the time, no scars or birthmarks, pretty poor set of teeth. Tattoo on left forearm.

What?

Tattoo on left forearm. Crest in maroon and blue and the words "Aston Villa Forever".

Thank Christ, a clue. A genuine bloody clue.

Well, things were different in the football world then, young man. These days most Manchester United fans live at least two hundred miles from Old Trafford, preferably in London or Peking, but back in the sixties, you were obliged to support your local team, which was a bloody cross to bear if you happened to be born in Wales. Cardiff, Swansea or bloody Newport.

My point is, that back then, anyone with an Aston Villa tattoo came from Birmingham. No doubt about it.

Well, I was on the phone to Birmingham CID straight away. We had a dead Brummy down here, did they have anyone matching the description?

They got back to me within the hour.

Carl Wood, bachelor aged thirty-five, fitter at Ford's Sellyoak factory. Went on holiday in early June and never showed up back at work. Reported missing by his married sister, who thought he'd gone on a coach trip to North Wales or somewhere. Five feet ten, brown hair and eyes, with a tattoo of Aston Villa FC on his left forearm.

This was going to mean a nasty trip down for the sister, but I thought I was finally beginning to see a glimmer or two of light at the end of the tunnel.

I just hoped it wasn't an approaching train.

Bloody hell, is that the time? I promised to meet the wife after her Book Club meeting. We'll have to leave it there. Next Tuesday good for you?

By the way, The Mail is still planning to serialise my memoirs, eh? It's just that I haven't seen hide nor hair of it in the paper. No that I read it myself, but the wife quite likes it.

Well, yes, I suppose it's best to have it finished before we start to unleash it upon the public. And, after all, I've had the advance.

Tuesday it is then.

Hello again, young man. Yes, but make it a brandy and soda, I don't want to end up maudlin again on the gin.

Now, we'd just identified the second corpse, hadn't we. Poor old Carl Wood from Birmingham. The Aston Villa supporter.

Well, his sister came down on the Tuesday on the train. Can't remember the name. It wasn't Wood, she was a married lady. We did the best we could for her, sent a car to Cardiff Central and drove her down to Barry. Same old routine with a WPC and the trip to Barry General. No, I still didn't go, Call me squeamish, but I always hated all that stuff.

She was back soon enough, all red-eyed and trying to keep things under control. I let the WPC sit in with us, just in case the lady needed comforting. And besides, it was never a good idea to be alone with a female witness. WPC Jane Langdon. I do remember her name. Same one who'd helped us in the search at "Skibbereen". Nice girl. It seemed she'd done well at the Hospital, caring sort of person. It helps sometimes in this job ... in that job I mean.

Yes, it was definitely Carl. What on earth had happened. He was such a quiet bloke. Stabbed to death on his holidays. What was it all about? Why Carl? Was it those Mods and Rockers?

It's a bugger sometimes this job. Well, I mean it was a bugger sometimes. Having to ask questions when people are at their lowest ebb. Used to make me feel such a swine, I'll tell you. But it had to be done.

So, had Carl been down to Barry before?

She had no idea, they hadn't seen each other that often, she was married and living in West Bromwich now, and since their parents died they hadn't met up very often. The odd phone call. He'd told her he was coming down to Wales, but she'd thought he meant North Wales. First she'd known about it was when she'd rung his digs and the landlady'd said he'd never come back. She'd rung Ford's then, and they'd said the same thing.

It was no use asking her where he'd been staying down here, since she'd never even known he'd been down here. No, no idea about girlfriends in Barry. He'd been married once, but his wife had run off with somebody or other. He'd never talked about any girls since then. Of course, she had absolutely no idea why someone might want to stick a knife into him. I showed her the photo of the dead girl, but she shook her head at once.

Did he have any enemies? What a bloody arsehole question that is, eh? Who do you know who's got bloody enemies who'd track him down from Birmingham to the wilds of Glamorgan to stick a knife in him. Still, we always ask it, and they always shake their heads. No, this panel beater, or whatever, hadn't incurred the wrath of any Sicilian secret societies or Chinese Tongs. As far as we could ascertain.

We'd asked her to bring a photo of her brother down, and she'd remembered it. A happy smiling bloke he looked, it had been taken at her wedding. I promised to let her have it back, once we'd had some copies made.

For some reason, she wanted to know where he'd been found, so I told her about the Graveyard. Oddly enough that brought a smile to her face.

"Carl would have liked that, he was always mad about steam trains. He's got a big set at home. Or he did have, I suppose."

It seemed that she knew nothing useful at all, so we gave her our sincere condolences, put her back in a car to Cardiff Central and she took the train back to Birmingham. Well, I assume she did. For all I know she took the train to London and embarked on a career as an exotic dancer .... but probably not.

No, I'll never make a comedian.

Another lot of rather dull routine stuff needed to be done now, and I still wasn't going to be doing any of it. That's what constables were for. Two of them were given copies of the photo of Carl Wood and despatched to show it round every hotel, guest house, caravan site and campsite in Barry.

Two more were told off to contact the offices of every coach company that worked between Birmingham and Barry and see if they'd sold a ticket to a Carl Wood. If he'd come down on the train, we were well stuffed, there was pretty much no chance that anyone would recognise a passenger who'd bought a ticket at Birmingham New Street two or three weeks ago. Still, it probably wasn't that important how he'd got down here, we knew he had somehow or other.

The first results to come in were a waste of time. The Birmingham coach companies didn't issue tickets with names on, so we'd have to start flashing the photo around again. I posted a copy up to the Birmingham CID, and sent the constables back to the coach offices down here to show it about.

Then we had some positive news. The Seaview guesthouse on Cadoxton Road recognised the photo as the bloke who's stayed with them for a week in early June. He was due to stay two weeks, but he'd gone out one night and not come back, so they'd assumed that his plans had changed.

I went down there. Took Sergeant Llewellyn along. Never liked to drive myself if I could find someone else to do it.

Mr and Mrs Something ran the place, and they weren't the brightest pennies in the pile. They hadn't bothered advising us of the disappearance of their guest .... after all, he'd paid the two weeks in advance. None of their business if he went home early. Yes, like lots of people go home and leave all their clothes behind. They'd put his stuff into the box room until he came back for it. Probably some family emergency.

Never underestimate human stupidity, son. Mind you, you work for The Mail, so you'll know all about that.

Just a little joke, that's all.

DS Llewellyn and I went through his stuff. Not much of it. one cheap suitcase. Underwear clean, underwear soiled. Socks similar, shirts similar. One pair sandals. One bathing costume. Washing and shaving kit. Toothbrush and toothpaste. One Agatha Christie novel. Ten Little ...... er .....one Agatha Christie novel. Everything else he'd been wearing, I suppose.

And.

One return ticket to Birmingham on Acocks Green Coaches.

Well, we were making progress. I wasn't sure in what direction, but we were finding stuff out. Back to the station we went. I had some telephone calls to make.

As it turned out, I received one first, from the Pontypridd Police. Their enquiries had failed to trace any missing Anna Rodriguez, Jean Rodriguez, or indeed any missing young lady answering to the description given. Well, as I'd said it was a pretty forlorn hope, but we had to try everything. That's the way it is, shine a light into every corner and see what's lurking there. Generally nothing.

My turn at the phone. I got the number of Acocks Green Coaches from Directory Enquiries and called them. It seemed they did a regular run to Barry in the holiday season, and, in fact, their coach was down here at the moment, ready to drive back up to Birmingham the following day. The coach would be parked on the Island coach park. The drivers always stayed at the same guest house, "Mon Repos" on Tenby Street down on the Island.

Off we went again, the good Detective Sergeant and myself. Nice enough place "Mon Repos" looked, run by a Mrs Whobloodyknows. Fat woman, I remember that. The drivers were actually having their evening meal at the time, so we waited half an hour till they came out. No, I dunno why either, maybe I was feeling kind that day. Maybe I fancied a sit down and a glass of lager from the residents' bar. Out they came anyway and we showed them the warrant cards and took them into the residents' lounge.

Introductions all round. You'll remember our names, I dare say. Charlie Timms and Sidney Harris were the drivers. I dunno, I can't really remember them all that well and I'm no good on descriptions. Big chaps. Brown hair. Fortyish. Elvis quiffs, so basically they looked like bus drivers. Never understood why so many bus drivers have Elvis hairstyles. Looked a little rough round the edges to me, but you can't judge a book by its cover, eh? Though funnily enough, that's where they write the description of what's in the book, don't they?

Out came the photo of poor old Carl Wood. Their eyes widened. Much nodding from the two drivers. Yes, they remembered driving him down about three weeks or so ago. Nice cove, gave them a shilling tip.

God, five pence, son.

Worth having back then, a shilling. They were sure

that he never went back up again. I showed them the return ticket, and the date on it. They shrugged. Head office didn't send them a list of passengers, they just picked up whoever was at the bus stop, checked their tickets and let them on. Anyway, even if they had been given a list, what were they supposed to do if someone didn't turn up? Search the backstreets of Barry for them?

Fair point.

I had one more question. How come there were two drivers on the bus.

Well, basically, because it was a bloody long way from Barry to Birmingham. Remember. son, this was back in the days before there were motorways all over the country. It took forever to get anywhere.

Yes, fair point, even with motorways it still bloody does. Thank God, I don't have to drive very far these days.

Acocks Green Coaches were proud of their safety record, and always put two drivers on each coach. It was a new firm, been going two years and never a hint of an accident. Every two hours, they changed places and a fresh pair of hands took the wheel. Timms and Harris, it seemed, were the regulars on this particular route. Good pals and valued clients at "Mon Repos."

Did they have friends in Barry?

Not really, but they'd pop down to the promenade or the funfair from time to time, or have their evening meal in one of the restaurants on the island.

Pubs?

No, they weren't drinkers at all. Instant dismissal to be caught with drink on their breath when driving a coach for Acocks Green.

Girlfriends?

Not down here. Timms had a wife and a kid up in Brum, while Harris was....between girls.

I showed then the photo of the dead girl. Shoulders were shrugged, neither of them had ever seen her as far as they knew. Was she the dead prostitute?

Well, I suppose they read the papers. We thanked them for their time wished them *bong voyarge* back to Birmingham and took our leave.

So there we were. I knew how Carl Wood had travelled down from Birmingham, I knew where he'd stayed, and I knew that he'd never used his return ticket.

Though, I suppose that finding him stabbed to death in the Barry Graveyard might have been thought of as a pretty big clue to the third thing.

Seem to remember sitting in the car outside with Llewellyn trying to make sense of the whole thing. A mystery woman strangled and a car-fitter stabbed in peaceful Barry Island just seemed so unlikely. Llewellyn was a bright enough chap, made Chief Inspector last I heard, but in those days he was always pretty quiet and respectful. Maybe too respectful to toss in an idea from time to time, but he was solid and dependable. Like a wall, so I tried bouncing an idea or two off him, to see what they sounded like out loud. One of them in particular bounced rather nicely, so I held on to it. Perhaps another chat to the Super seemed indicated on the morrow.

Yes, I know it's dragging on a bit, son, but real Police work can do that. I like the fictional stuff, but that's what it is, made up. And it has its rules, doesn't it? The killer has to be someone who plays a major role in the story, and it's just a question of deciding which of the six it is. Well, Barry had forty-two thousand residents, plus a pretty large floating population of tourists in the summer months, so I'm sorry if I haven't been able to narrow it down for your readers. Chances were a hundred to one that the killer would be a complete stranger when, or if, we caught him. So no, it wasn't Sergeant Llewellyn gone mental, my long-lost brother or any of that stuff. And it didn't seem as if the case was likely to be solved inside the right number of pages either.

Let's get back to it.

Next day I went to see Superintendent Watkins again, got offered more tea. Custard Creams this time. Perks of rank. I told him my theory.

Course I'll tell you, no sense being all enematic about it, you're the one doing the writing.

It seemed pretty obvious that Jean Rodriguez (we'll stick with that name) had been a prozzie, whore, harlot, worker in the sex-industry, doxie, professional bedwarmer or whatever your preferred PC term is. She'd been obliged to peddle her body to make a living, poor soul. She'd been known to work the promenade area, and it didn't take too much imagination to suppose that Mr Carl Wood, bereft of his conjuring rights since the departure of his wife, might have been feeling the urge. Perhaps fate brought them together, an offer was made and accepted and a bargain struck.

Which left them with the slight problem of the venue. Their respective boarding houses would have been a non starter, the Barry Island Hotel wasn't the sort of establishment to offer rooms by the hour. I've no doubt that, as with most of her ....fellow workers ... Miss Rodriguez knew of a room nearby, but perhaps Mr Wood had something more unusual in mind. His sister said he was keen on trains, so what more interesting than to do the deed actually in a train. The Graveyard's only a short walk from the Promenade after all.

"Bloody Hell," was the Super's considered response to that.

Now of course, that could just have been my dirty mind working overtime. It could equally well have been that they got talking at the ice-cream stall, discovered a mutual interest in steam trains and popped over there with their notebooks to jot down some numbers. Though we hadn't found any notebooks.

In the end, it didn't matter which, though I knew which option seemed more likely. They'd gone there together to do something.

The Super nodded.

Well, whatever they went there for, they bumped into something they weren't expecting. Something big and nasty. For sure not just another courting couple, kids smashing windows, scrap metal thieves. Something big enough and nasty enough to warrant cold blooded murder to stop them telling anybody about it.

The Super was leaning forward in his chair now and I went on.

Something had been going on in The Graveyard that night for sure, but we had no idea what.

The Super sat back in his chair.

"Is that it, Williams? I can't see that it gets us anywhere. We've no idea what, why or, most importantly, who?"

He had a good point there of course, but I wasn't quite finished. Maybe whatever had happened might happen again some time. Maybe it was worth keeping a watch on The Graveyard for a while.

He thought about it, but shook his head.

"Look at the size of the place, we'd need half a dozen men and even then we'd probably miss it. Might just have been someone after their money?"

Well, I doubted that, the fashion for mugging hadn't reached our shores (another wonderful American invention) and I really couldn't see cold-blooded double murder for the few pounds they might have been carrying between them. The sexual motive was out too, since the lady hadn't been touched. No, since you mention it, the gentleman hadn't been molested either. I assume. I'm sure the Doctor would have mentioned it.

To be fair, the Super was decent enough about it.

"You've done a pretty good job on this Williams, but I think you've gone as far as you can with what precious little evidence you had. I don't think it's worth throwing more man-hours at this unless we get some fresh leads come in."

He was right of course, standing half a dozen constables down there twenty-four hours a day was a fairly desperate idea. It looked like this one wasn't going to be solved.

Yes maybe it is time for another, I'm drying up again. Not used to being allowed to talk this long without interruption, not with my wife. Hahahaha. No, son, that bit doesn't go in the paper, I've told you, she's been known to read it.

I wasn't at all happy. No, I couldn't fault the Super's decision, but I just kept thinking that I could have tried harder. Maybe I'd missed something along the way. Yes, the "vital clue" we're always looking for, the crushed cigarette end, the mysterious footprint, but there was nothing.

Of course, these days we'd hold a re-enactment, maybe put it on the telly. Crimewatch. Get a couple of actors to dress up as the victim, shoot the whole thing with some low lighting and mysterious shadowy figures doing the evil deed.

"Did that jog your memory at all? Have you any recollection of seeing two young people brutally slaughtered last Wednesday evening? Did anyone you know come home covered in blood that night and give you a knife to hide?"

Hadn't been thought of back then, and I'm pretty sure it would have got us nowhere. Makes for good telly, but lousy Police work, I'm afraid.

The Super was right, there was nowhere to go, so it was time to leave it. Not close it, son. We never close a murder case, some of them get solved twenty years later. Lots more these days, what with that ENA stuff.

I think that must have been Thursday and I had a weekend off coming up, so Friday was probably a paperwork day. The Press had got bored of reporting the lack of progress, and nobody seemed to recognise Jean Rodriguez from the photo they'd printed. I'd sent it to the Cardiff boys and to some of the English ports too, just in case they had nothing better to do than flash it around the prostitutes on their patch. Seemed pointless, at best I'd just get a different name.

I left early and went across the road to The Swan, which was by way of being the Coppers' pub, since it was so close to the nick. That WPC Jane Langdon was in there too. She looked prettier out of uniform and with her hair down. Nice figure I seem to recall. Never liked them skinny, and she was nicely covered, but no sign of fat. Fraternising amongst the ranks wasn't really encouraged, but I thought a port and lemon or two for her wouldn't cause a national scandal, so we had a little chat for an hour or two.

About the case, about how it was all but dead, about people we both knew around Barry, about what we had planned for the evening meal, about how the Barry Hotel was meant to do a good steak, about perhaps driving up there. My treat.

Taking advantage? Might be seen that way now, I suppose. But you never met the lady. I bet no-one took advantage of her in her life.

A good steak it was indeed, and a fair enough lager to go with it too. I don't really ever remember anyone drinking wine at all, it wasn't really a British thing. Those poofy Frogs were always swilling it to wash down their horrible snails. My dad helped pull their frogs' legs out of the fire in '44.

Sorry, I'm from a bygone age, young man, cut out what you need to. Don't want to offend our European cousins. Or any snails or frogs, come to that.

She was a bright girl, well educated. Stayed on at school a couple of years longer than I had. We talked a bit more about the dead girl, then some more about mutual acquaintances, the job, where we saw ourselves going. Films we'd seen, music we'd liked. She'd dropped the "Sir" by now. Seemed foolish not to.

Anyway, an enjoyable dinner for two, but we both knew it was never likely to go anywhere, the difference in ranks made it a bad idea.

Made it an even worse idea when I woke up next to her in my bed on the Saturday morning. Maybe she just wanted to try out her new Pill. Tried it out another couple of times that morning too, as I remember. Yeeeeeeessssss .... I do remember.

Don't worry about cutting that out.

No, it won't upset Mrs Williams, she is Mrs Williams now. Not so much of the twice every morning these days though. Well yes, that bit you better had cut out!

She left after lunch since she was working that afternoon. I think we both knew it might be a mistake. Still, you don't always learn from your mistakes, do you son?

As you'd expect, I was feeling a lot happier about life in general, though still a little disappointed that my big case had come to nothing.

It was another sunny Barry afternoon, so I took myself off to the Island to enjoy the amenities offered by South Wales' leading holiday destination. A nice swim, an hour or two on the beach with a James Bond book and a bottle of suncream (ahead of my time I must have been, but I didn't fancy sunburn), a few shots on the rifle range to win another cheap china ornament for Mother's mantelpiece and an ice-cream while I watched the Guinness clock.

That? It was a big clock on the promenade with lots of little figures who'd pop out and dance or sing when it struck the hour. Penguins, Swiss girls, I dunno what all. Daft, but it always made me laugh. No. I suppose it's long gone. Like most things I remember from those days. Haven't been back in forty years. Best not, eh?

Well, it was all meant to take my mind of things, but there was no chance. I just couldn't leave it alone. As soon as the clock finished, I walked through the funfair, across the road and the hundred yards or so up to the Graveyard.

It wasn't open of course, but I didn't feel like going in there anyway. I just stood and stared at them. The giants. Couldn't think of another word for them Just giants, whose time was over. Slowly rusting away.

Rows of them, huge, silent, dead, telling me nothing.

I gave it up, gave one last wave to my old friend "Pride of Mansfield" and turned to go.

And then I didn't go. I stood there and stared at the handsome, tired old warrior and I saw the answer written right in front of my eyes.

Call myself a bloody detective? A child of six could have solved it.

I had to make sure, so I walked round the fence until I found a Williams-sized hole and pushed my way through. I had the place to myself that afternoon as I walked across to the second row and carefully made my way down until I reached the engine where we'd found the dead girl.

Yes. I was right.

I do believe I'd got it.

Showing up at the Nick on the evening of my day off certainly caused some raised eyebrows, but I needed to see the Super at once. Fortunately he hadn't gone home already. I seem to remember that my being off duty and his being off home soon was excuse enough for a little splash each from the bottom drawer bottle. A nice drop of whisky he kept too. He was as curious as anyone, but waited for me to start.

"It's the bloody buffers. That's how they're doing it."

Well, no doubt he wondered who was doing what and which bloody buffers, but he let me go on.

The first time we were down there I'd seen 2/10 chalked on the buffer of the first old loco in the place. I thought it was something to do with its date of arrival or intended date of scrapping, but it was neither of those. Where did we find the body?"

He still said nothing.

"In an engine called "Sir Richard Grenville. On the second siding, tenth one down. 2/10"

"So someone was trying to tell us where to find her?"

"No, they'd just dial 999. Would have taken us years to figure that out. It was a rendezvous. Telling whoever was coming where the meeting was to be. By the time we did the search last Sunday, it had changed to 5/12. Fifth row along, twelfth loco down. I've just been down there again and it says 3/18.

That's what tipped me off that it couldn't be a date, it was a place. Directions."

"So they'll be meeting in row three, eighteenth engine down?"

"I don't think so, I think we've missed that one. I think whoever gets there first writes the venue on the buffer for the second guy to read. They've just been too careless to rub it off afterwards. Or maybe they both assume that the other one did it."

He was thinking hard now, and I've no doubt he was getting to the same conclusions I was. Regular meetings in a very out of the way place, between parties who had to communicate by chalk marks. Parties who clearly couldn't just telephone each other. Parties desperate enough to resort to deadly violence if interrupted.

"Drugs of some sort, Williams?"

I thought so. These days it would be the first conclusion you'd jump to, but the world was a different place in those days. Of course, there'd always been addicts, and quite a few of the rich and famous were known to indulge, but it wasn't really a street level problem. Communications weren't so good, of course. People didn't jet all over the world, so we didn't see anywhere near as much of it.

Of course, there were Customs posts at all the ports, but nothing like as rigorous as now. No sniffer dogs, body scanners, X-rays and shoe searches. Clever boys could bring stuff in easily enough.

"Coming in or going out, would you think Williams?"

I favoured coming in, though it would be the same system either way. A meeting and an exchange of some stuff. Heroin it always used to be. Cocaine was not unheard of, but it hadn't reached the popularity it has now.

I couldn't see the money changing hands, that was probably done via banks. The banks didn't bother keeping an eye on transactions back then. The Proceeds Of Crime Act was forty years in the future. A suitcase full of pound notes would be much harder to hide than the white goods. And they'd have to be moved elsewhere pretty sharpish, since South Wales wasn't exactly a hotbed of addiction Off to some big city probably.

The Super was still nodding

"How do you think they're being brought in, Williams?"

Well, I had a theory about that too. There had been three different rendezvous markings in the last two weeks, Possibly more of course. I hadn't been down every day. That seemed to rule out big oil tankers, since they didn't tend to arrive in Barry Docks with that sort of frequency And besides, to get couriers working on ships owned by different companies wouldn't have been easy.

But there was one type of ship showing up very regularly at the moment. Most of them owned by one company, and all of them coming from the Caribbean, pretty close to the USA, and with no shortage of drug availability.

The Banana Boats.

Best not name the firm involved son, even though this was all a long time ago. They're still in the business, and they weren't responsible for a few bad apples amongst the bananas. Apples, bananas? No? Suit yourself.

"But why in God's name haven't they changed the meeting place Williams? They must know we'd be far more interested down there after finding the bodies."

Very probably they couldn't, was my answer to that one. With the boats at sea. they could hardly send a message out. "Rendezvous changed. Take drugs to 42 Holton Road instead," could they? Chances are that the British end of the chain wouldn't even know the name of the bloke who was bringing the stuff in. But I was pretty sure they would be changing it, as soon as they could, so we'd need to be looking smart if we wanted to catch them in the act.

The Super had one final question.

"Where do you think they're shipping the stuff off to,

Williams?"

I told him.

He looked thoughtful again.

"This might be just a little too big for us, you know, and some other forces might be wanting to get involved. The whole thing might end up being taken out of our hands. I'll need to refer it up. Wouldn't surprise me if it was dealt with at Chief Constable level."

I wasn't happy about that at all, son. My big case, I'd finally got somewhere with it and now it was about to be taken off me.
I didn't bother mentioning how I felt. In this job you learn to roll with the punches rather than kick against the ...... well, you learn to accept things.

Anyway, it seemed that neither of us was going home just yet. He had phone calls to make, and I had more information to gather.

I wasn't really dressed for the part of a senior policeman, wearing a pair of khaki slacks and an open necked shirt, but I hadn't expected to be working. In the circumstances I thought a bit of official uniformed presence might add an air of authority to things. There weren't a lot of choices on a Saturday evening, so I took the obvious one.

"Langdon, can you drive?"

"Yes, sir."

Well done girl, not a flicker of a smile, not a twitched eyebrow out of place. She had class, that young lady.

"Good, drive me down to the Dock Office, if you would."

We took one of the Anglias I seem to remember. Bloody horrible cars, looked like they'd been cut out of cardboard by an eight-year old. Joogle yourself a photo to put in the paper, young man. Nice unfussy driver she was. A bit more indecisive in her later years, but you won't be needing to put that in, will you. Touchy about her driving she is these days.

I had a pretty good idea of what I'd learn down at the Docks office, but I wasn't going to leave anything to chance. This looked like getting big, and all my Ts were going to be firmly dotted. In we went together and I showed my warrant card, though the uniform next to me seemed persuasion enough for the little bloke behind the counter. More than happy to help,

Officer.

I was right. There'd been a boat come in two Wednesdays ago, another one the Monday after, then the following Friday, then Wednesday, then Friday again. The next one was due in on Monday. They generally only stayed a night or two in Barry. Time was money, and empty boats were no use to anyone. In, unload, bugger off.

She drove me back to the nick. Said nothing the whole time, which was probably the right thing to do. Business and pleasure should be kept apart I've always said. Rarely took my own advice though, thank God.

I went back to my desk. There was a note from the Super saying he'd be expecting me in tomorrow, and he'd be there too. Bang went his golf at Penarth. I tried a few trunk calls, but there was nothing doing. Everyone had gone home. Places worked shorter hours in those days. Barry had an early closing day, so none of the shops opened on a Wednesday afternoon at all. And you could forget trying to buy anything on a Sunday except your newspaper, though the gift shops on the Island were open in the season. Supermarkets? There were precious few around, and they were open the same hours as everyone else. Illegal to open on a Sunday. Shops Act.

Where was I? Yes, business was over for the day and I wouldn't be getting an answer now till Monday.

But maybe there was another way to find out. I looked up a number in the Barry Directory and dialled. Just four numbers . Mine used to be 2943 .... funny the things you remember, isn't it. I got an answer quickly enough.

Yes, of course she remembered me.

Yes, tomorrow.

Yes, Tuesday.

I asked a few more questions, but she had to look those up. I waited and she was back soon. I wrote down the answers and hung up. I made some notes with a pencil, cross-checked dates and times. It fitted. Of course, it could just be a coincidence, especially at that time of year, but at least I knew my theory was possible.

I made one final call to the Records Office. I'd get a reply in the morning.

I was almost beginning to feel like a detective.

I was also beginning to feel hungry, so I got a PC to drive me to the chippy and then off home. Not WPC Langdon. At the time I wasn't quite ready for lightning to strike twice, and I also thought I might need a full night's sleep. I took a sleeping draught to make sure. Something medically approved and highly effective.

Johnny Walker Red Label.

One more, I think we're nearly there. Make it brandy this time, because the rest of the story is enough to make me morose without the assistance of gin.

This was the Sunday wasn't it? I was in bright and early, but not quite as early as Superintendent Watkins, who naturally wanted to see me. The news was pretty much what I'd expected, but I was still a little bit cheesed off.

"I'm sorry, Williams, but it's out of our hands now. They're sending down a specialised Task Force with a Superintendent Briggs in charge. They'll be here this afternoon, and I want you to liaise with them and give them everything we've got."

I nodded, then I told him what I'd discovered from the Dock Office and the phone call. He nodded too. I told him about the call I'd had back from Records.

"It could be couldn't it? Might well make sense. That's where the Task Force is coming down from. Apparently there'll be no arrests here, surveillance only. They want to follow this all the way up and get the big fish, not just the sprats."

I could understand that well enough, but I kept hearing the words of the two young ladies the other night, so I pointed out that there were two unsolved murders on our patch tied in with all this.

"I know Williams, and I'm damned sure that if we can break this whole thing, we'll have some answers about the murders too. They're not going to be forgotten about. I promise you."

I was far from convinced, but I had a job to do. I went back and collected everything I had, everything I knew, everything I'd guessed and everything I thought and put it all into the one file. Then I went to Church.

Yes, that surprised you sonny, as well it might. I've never been much of a believer, but I did like the hymns, and the silences, and occasionally a good sermon. Long time ago now, mind you. Not sure I've been in thirty years except for weddings and funerals. But that day I went. Don't remember much about it, but maybe it calmed me down a little. It wouldn't have done to have got emotional those two days.

Lunch in the canteen, I think. I can remember looking for WPC Langdon and feeling a little disappointed that she wasn't about. A bad sign that was and I ticked myself off for it. Then I decided to forgive myself. She was a nice piece of goods. I was entitled to a little consolation. Still, as I said, she wasn't there.

Mid-afternoon it was when the Special Task Force arrived in a plain minibus. They weren't at all what I was expecting.
For a start they were a real scruffy bunch of blokes .... though there was one girl I think, maybe two ..... not very well dressed, some in need of a haircut or a shave. And the blokes were even worse!

Alright son, I'll cut the jokes.

Even Briggs wasn't wearing a tie, some sort of blazer and open-necked shirt. He was bloody young for a Super, not much more than forty. Still, I suppose in Special Task Forces people get ahead a little quicker.

Anyway, he and his crew crowded into a briefing room and I told them what we'd got, and one or two of my guesses. There was a Banana Boat due in the following afternoon, and the contacts were in town too. I could have been badly wrong on the contacts though, but there was only one way to find out. If I was right, the handover would be made tomorrow, probably just before twilight as they wouldn't want to be waving too many torches about. By then any possible trainspotters or kids would be at home having their tea and the place would be as quiet as a real graveyard.

Briggs seemed pretty impressed by my reasoning .... at any rate he did a lot of nodding. Then he took over.

This would be a surveillance only operation, not even particularly close surveillance, since they had a fair idea of the people involved, and where everyone was going. They were also going to have a couple of watchers with binoculars dug in nearby, and possible locations would be scouted out that evening. What DI Wilson (thank you very much!) had said tied in with their own intelligence. With a little luck, they'd be able to break up the whole ring. Off they went to do whatever it was they had to do.

Be fair to Briggs, he treated me decently enough. It was his operation now, but he was highly impressed with my work, and he'd see to it that I got full credit for it. As a courtesy, if I wanted to join one of the watching groups .....

No thanks. I'm pretty big and conspicuous, and I have an unfortunate tendency to look like a policeman. Besides which, though I kept this bit to myself, I had a couple of days off to catch up on. I'd taken a peek at the duty rota and seen that WPC Langdon was also off .... and the Theatre Royal was showing the new James Bond film.

As it turned out she was something of a cinema fan, and particularly liked James Bond, so she was happy to accept my offers.

Thunderballs.

No, son. That was the name of the film.

Anyway, my son, that was the end of my involvement in the Graveyard Case. I know, anti-climate wasn't it. By rights DI Williams should have been the hero of the hour, burst in on the merchants of misery *in fragrante derelicto* and slapped on the cuffs.

Doesn't always work out like the books, eh?

Don't worry, I won't leave your readers in suspenders, of course I heard about it all afterwards. The Super had me in a week or so later and told me the full story. Turns out I'd been pretty damned close.

One of the scruff squad was hanging around the dock gates late that Monday afternoon, when he sees a darky come out and start walking off towards the Island causeway

What? What am I supposed to call him? He wasn't African or American ... he was West Indian, can I say that? Alright.

Anyway, that's unusual in itself, as those boys used to stay pretty close to the docks, as they weren't all that welcome in the town pubs. Different times son, different times.

Can't say boys either? Whatever you say son, just put in the right words for me. Dinosaur, bloody dinosaur, that's what I am.

The ... West Indian Gentleman made his way past another scruff at the end of the causeway and headed down towards the Graveyard. Sun was just beginning to go down. By this time he was being watched from a couple of vantage points by other scruffs with binoculars. He gets to the graveyard fence, finds himself a hole and wriggles through, with a bit of difficulty, as he's not too slim. Walks up to my old friend "Pride of Mansfield" sees the 5/25 chalked on the bumper, remembers to rub it off and sets off to the fifth siding. Walks down and, twenty five engines later, he climbs onto the footplate.

Ten minutes or so later, out he comes, looking a little slimmer this time (apparently there were long plastic bags of the stuff wrapped round his waist .... amateurish, but the Customs boys .... er .... gentlemen had been tipped off not to be too vigilant).

Another ten minutes later, out come two men wearing open neck shirts and slacks, one of them carrying a duffle bag. Duffle bag? It's a sports bag you used to carry over your shoulder, before they invented Adididias. Some of the scruff squad watch them on their way, but there's no real need, as they know where they're going since they followed them down.

Back to "Mon Repos" on Tenby Street.

That's it, Charlie and Sidney, the two Birmingham coach drivers.
Well, I dunno, it was no more than a hunch at best. I'd never come across a firm that put two drivers on a bus, and the timings fitted. No more than that. Oh, and a little check of the Criminal Records that revealed they'd both been inside, GBH and Assault & Battery respectively.

Well, that was pretty much job done at the Barry end. Applause for DI Williams, who'd been right all the way along. More by luck than judgement, I'll admit.

The West Indian gentleman was allowed to rejoin his

ship, though I believe the Jamaican authorities were waiting for him when he got home. Part of the Empire in those days, of course.

Charlie and Sidney drove their bus back up to Birmingham on the Tuesday, with a couple of the scruff squad as extra passengers, and the West Midlands Police ready to greet them. As it happened, they raided the whole Acocks Green Coaches set-up, and found that most of their routes were to coastal towns and operating the same deal. In fact the entire organisation was just a front for a nationwide distribution scheme.

They smashed it, heavy prison sentences all round. I definitely got a big boost in my career from that, and my transfer to the Met was approved six months later.

Well done me, eh.

Ah yes, the murders.

Not such a good result really.

We had no real evidence you see. We went up to Birmingham. I took DS Llewellyn and interviewed both the bus drivers. Harris and Timms. At first they denied everything.

I told them what I thought. They'd been safely in the "Sir Richard Whatsit" quietly transferring the stuff from the long bags into the duffle bag, when Jean

Rodriguez had climbed up onto the footplate and maybe given a little scream. One of them had strangled her, the other one had chased after Carl Wood and stabbed him.

I took them one at a time, of course, told them we'd seen the 2/10 on the buffer, knew that was their way of communicating, so could place them at the scene. Neither of them would confess. Sat there smoking and smirking.

I tried a little trickery. Told each of them that the other had turned Queen's evidence and was accusing his mate of both murders. No, you surely could not do that today, but things were a little more lax then. None of that PACE stuff. Harris laughed in my face, told me exactly where to go.

Timms wasn't quite so tough and he started to weaken. Then he gave me a story. I was pretty sure the two of them were playing silly buggers with me, and had cooked it up between them but this was the story.

It wasn't him, and it wasn't Harris. It was the dar .... the West Indian gentleman. A different one, of course. Off a different boat.

I was right, she'd climbed up on the footplate and squealed when she'd seen them. As soon as he saw her, the dar .... the West Indian gentleman had grabbed her scarf, pulled it tight and strangled her. All over in seconds. Then he'd jumped down off the footplate, chased after Wood and stuck a knife in him. Timms never even knew he had a knife.

Naturally, he had no idea of his name, and the description he gave could have been eighty percent of the male population of the West Indies. Black, medium height, about thirty.

Bollocks, the whole thing.

I had no idea how long it takes to strangle a woman, but surely Wood could have got away in that time? And if a man's carrying a knife and uses it on one victim, why not the other? And then there were those bruises on her arms where somebody held her, probably while someone else was killing her.

I wasn't having it, and wanted to charge them both with willful murder and hope for a decent judge and jury. The Public Prosecutor wouldn't wear it. I was furious, but it did me no good. In the end they both got an extra seven years for accessory to murder. It was something, but it wasn't enough. Maybe there's some Jamaican still walking around scot free over there. Or even over here now, the way the immigration's gone. Maybe my successors are trying to sort out his kids, eh?

There was no point me making a fuss, though I still think we could have got the bastards convicted for murder. As it was, neither of them ever came out again. I took an interest in their progress, and I can't say I shed a tear when one of them had a heart attack five years in and the other died of cancer eighteen months later. Can't remember which way round it was .... you could find out.

So, maybe after all I sort of kept my promise to Jenny and Sue. I know I did the best I could.

I do know that the Graveyard's not there any more, one of my grandsons looked it up for me on the Intraweb last weekend. All those locomotives have gone, But apparently eighty percent of them never went for scrap after all. They were sold on to enthusiasts' groups and restored. A lot of them still running to this day.

That's the nearest we'll be getting to a happy ending.

As for the rest of it, no neat conclusion I'm afraid. There often isn't.

There is one thing that I still think about though, even after all this time.

From that day to this, as far as I know, nobody ever came forward to tell us who the bloody Hell Jean Rodriguez was.

No, no more for me sonny, I'm off home. Maybe see you next time eh?

Jane? Come here a minute, love.

Look at this, from the Daily Mail. Apparently they've decided not to serialise my memoirs after all. What do they say, "rather too many of them appear to have downbeat, inconclusive endings with which our readers may not identify" "many of the characters do not seem interesting enough or fully developed" "quite often the identity of the murderer comes as a complete surprise."

Bastards, why not just print some bloody made up crime novel instead. Do they want the truth or not? After all the time I spent talking to them about that last case. You remember the bloody Graveyard murders? Yes, yes, that was the case. Long time ago, eh? Some good came out of it though, eh, my dear? Indeed it did.

Still, it's not all bad, they don't want the advance back. And they've sent a CD of the interviews. I got quite a few drinks out of that poor young chap they sent. Didn't know his arse from his elbow, silly sod.

Ah well, fancy a stroll along the prom? We could stop at the Red Lion? I'm told they do a nice steak there. And a decent glass of lager.

Printed in Great Britain
by Amazon.co.uk, Ltd.,
Marston Gate.